North Wales
Folk Tales for Children

Fiona Collins

Illustrated by Ed Fisher

The History Press

For Amber, because you like
listening to my stories,
from Fiona.

For Cousin Thelma, because you
told me stories to shorten the way,
from Ed.

(I especially remember the story
about the worms in the rain)

First published 2016

The History Press
97 St George's Place,
Cheltenham, Gloucestershire, GL50 3QB
www.thehistorypress.co.uk

Text © Fiona Collins, 2016
Illustrations © Ed Fisher, 2016

The right of Fiona Collins to be identified as the Author
of this work has been asserted in accordance with the
Copyright, Designs and Patents Act 1988.

British Library Cataloguing in Publication Data.
A catalogue record for this book is available from the British Library.

ISBN 978 0 7509 6427 2

Typesetting and origination by The History Press
Printed in Great Britain by TJ International Ltd, Padstow, Cornwall

CONTENTS

THE LAND OF THE STORIES

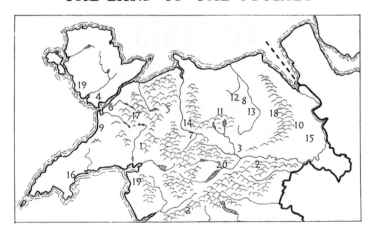

The numbers on the map are the numbers of the stories in this book. They show you where to find the places which are important in the stories. Some numbers are on the map twice, because there are two important places in that story. When place names are very different in Welsh and English, both are given.

ABOUT THE AUTHOR AND ILLUSTRATOR

Fiona has been a storyteller for twenty-five years, collecting and telling traditional tales from around the world. She especially loves the stories of North Wales, where she lives and works, telling stories and writing books … like this one.

Ed has lived in the same North Wales cottage for forty-three years, overlooking the Dee valley. It is an area of magic and wonder. Drawing is in his blood, as he is a fourth-generation artist. His grandfather, Josh Fisher, was a well-known landscape painter.

INTRODUCTION

Here are some of my favourite stories from North Wales. I hope you will like them too. They are folk tales and fairy tales – the kind of stories that nearly always begin 'Once Upon a Time' in English, 'Amser maith yn ôl' in Welsh.

Even though they aren't true stories, most of them are set in real places in North Wales. If you know the places, or can visit them, I think the stories will really come alive for you.

I asked some friends aged between 5 and 11 years old to read some of the stories while I was writing this book. I wanted to be sure that young readers would like them. Here are some of the things they said:

Alex said,

'Very exciting and strange …'

Mabel said,

'This is a good book.'

Jonty and Llion said,

'It wasn't too hard to read.'

Millie and Connie said,

'Very funny and good for children.
Well done!'

Aidan said,

'I like how you use real places.'

William liked the first story in the book because it has a happy ending. Mia and Angel gave the same story a score of nine and a half out of ten. They said, 'It would be good if there was a map for the locations.'

The map seemed like a really good idea, so Ed decided to make one to go with his beautiful drawings. We both hope you like his pictures and that they help you imagine the places and people in the stories.

These aren't my stories. They are old, old tales and many people tell them. In this book I've told them in my own way, the way I would tell them if you and I were sitting by a campfire, or in my living room. If you like them, why don't you tell them too? Tell them in *your* own way, in your own words. The great thing about these old, old stories is that no one can say to you, 'You're telling them wrong!'

Have fun reading this book,
and don't forget to live happily ever after.

Fiona Collins
May 2016

1

TWO DRAGONS

There are many stories about the great wizard Merlin. This is one of my favourites.

When Merlin was a boy, his full name was Myrddin ap Emrys, and he grew up in Caerfyrddin, which in English is called Carmarthen. Its Welsh name means Merlin's Castle. But Merlin had no castle there. In fact, he had no proper home.

His mother lived in a convent, with holy women who prayed all day and were not interested in children. And he had no father. Some people said his father was an evil spirit. Some said he was a good spirit. But Merlin didn't know, and if his mother knew she didn't tell him.

Merlin was not an ordinary boy, nor indeed a very happy one. Unkind people sometimes bully people who seem a bit different, and Merlin was very different, so he was often lonely or sad.

Although Merlin was still only young, he already had magic powers. So on the day that something strange began to happen, he knew what to do.

Some boys were playing with a ball, on the grass outside the city gate. Merlin wanted to join in, but the others wouldn't let him. They shouted, 'Go away, Merlin! You can't play. You haven't even got a father. Go away!'

Merlin knew it was no use arguing with them. He turned and went back through the city gate, back towards the convent where he lived with his mother and the silent sisters. But he hadn't walked far when he realised he was not alone. Someone was following him, staying in the shadows; keeping him in sight, but keeping out of his sight.

Merlin knew, by his magic, that this was a king's messenger, and that the king had sent the messenger to find a boy who never had a father. He knew why the king wanted such a boy, and he knew that he was the boy the king needed. So he wasn't afraid. He let the messenger follow him to the gate of the convent. When the gatekeeper saw Merlin's face through the bars on her window, she opened a little door in the gate and let him in, but she stopped the man who followed him, as Merlin knew she would.

'Strangers may not enter this house,' she said.

'Lady, I am on a king's quest and I carry a king's ring to prove it.'

The messenger held up a ring with a large jewel set in it, and showed it to the gatekeeper through the bars on the window. 'I have been sent to find a certain boy, and I believe that the boy who just went in is the one I am looking for.'

The old woman looked at the ring for a long time. Slowly, as though she did not really want to, she opened the little door just wide enough for the messenger to squeeze inside.

'Wait here, please,' she said. 'I will fetch the people you need to speak to.'

Merlin did not hear their conversation, but he knew how it would end. The nuns and his mother would agree to let him go to the king, waiting in the mountains of Snowdonia.

Sure enough, when the messenger rode out of the city and turned north, Merlin was sitting behind him on his great horse's back. They rode through Wales until they came to the high mountains: Snowdonia, which in Welsh is called The Place of Eagles, Eryri.

The king was standing at the top of a hill. All around him were the ruins of a tower: tools that were scattered, stones that were shattered, wood that had clattered to the ground. Behind him stood seven wise men. They looked frightened. Day after day, the king had asked them, 'Why does my tower keep falling down?' The wise men did not know. But if you are a king's wise man, you cannot tell him 'I don't know'. He won't be very pleased! So the seven not-very-wise men had made up an answer to his question.

Merlin rode behind the messenger.

'Your Majesty, you must find a boy who never had a father. You must kill him and bury his bones where you want to build your tower. Then your tower will stay strong. It will not fall down.'

They didn't know if this was the right answer to his question. They didn't care if it was the right answer. They thought it would be impossible for the king to find a boy who never had a father, so he would never know whether they were right or wrong.

But here was the messenger, and with him was a boy who never had a father … no wonder they looked frightened.

One person who didn't look frightened was Merlin. He walked right up to the king. He looked straight at him. Then he said, 'Your Majesty, I know why you have brought me here. But if you kill me and bury my bones, you will never find out why your tower keeps falling down. Ask your wise men what is under the ground here, and if they do not know, ask me, because I do.'

So the king turned to his wise men and asked them, 'What is under the ground here?'

They looked at the king, they looked at each other, they looked at the ground. They didn't know the answer, so they tried to guess, 'Earth, Your Majesty? Stones? Worms?'

The king looked at Merlin. Merlin shook his head.

'Your Majesty,' he said, 'just where you want to build your tower, there is an underground lake. If you don't believe me, tell your workers to dig there. You will see if I am right.'

The king's workers started to dig. It wasn't long until their spades broke through the roof of a cave. In it there was an underground lake.

Merlin spoke to the king, 'Your Majesty, ask your wise men what is under the lake, and if they do not know, ask me, because I do.'

So the king turned to his wise men and asked them, 'What is under the lake?'

They looked at the king, they looked at each other, they looked at the water. They didn't know the answer, so they tried to guess, 'Mud, your Majesty? Weed? Fish?'

The king looked at Merlin. Merlin shook his head.

'Your Majesty,' he said, 'under the lake, there is a great flat stone. If you don't believe me, tell your workers to drain the water out of the lake. You will see if I am right.'

The king's workers started to drain the water from the lake. Before long, the water was gone, and in the middle of the mud they all saw a great grey stone.

Merlin spoke to the king, 'Your Majesty, ask your wise men what is under the stone, and if they do not know, ask me, because I do.'

So the king turned to his wise men and asked them, 'What is under the stone?'

They looked at the king, they looked at each other, they looked at the stone. They didn't know the answer. They just shook their heads.

The king turned to Merlin.

'Your Majesty,' he said, 'under the stone, two dragons are curled up, fast asleep. All day they sleep, but at night they wake, and then they fight. Their battle destroys your tower each night. If you don't believe me, tell your workers to lift the stone. You will see if I am right.'

They lifted the stone out of the mud, and found two small sleeping dragons, curled up like piglets. One was red, the other was white. When the stone was moved and the light shone on them, they woke up. They opened their eyes, turned their heads, and saw each other. Then their eyes flashed, their teeth gnashed and their claws crashed. They spread their wings and rose up out of the hole in the ground. As they flew, they grew, until they were huge fiery shapes above the heads of the king, his wise men and his workers. They all crouched down in fear.

Only Merlin stood tall, watching the dragons as they began to fight, turning and whirling in the air, tearing with their claws and blasting fire from their jaws.

Merlin shouted out, 'Watch these dragons, and you will learn about the future! The red dragon is the dragon of Wales, and the white is the dragon of our enemies. They are fighting, and we will have to fight too.

Sometimes it will seem as though the red dragon will win, and sometimes the white will be stronger. But even if the red dragon is wounded, she will not die. Look now, and you will see if I am right!'

They all turned their faces up to the sky, and watched the fight. Just as Merlin had said, sometimes the red dragon seemed to be winning, sometimes the white. The flames and smoke and noise were terrible! Then the white dragon gave a great slash with its claws, and the red one seemed to fall out of the sky. The white dragon spread its wings and flew away. Everyone looked for the red dragon. It was nowhere to be seen.

Merlin spoke again, 'The red dragon is not dead, but she is wounded. She is the dragon of this land. Now she needs to rest and grow strong again. Then, when Wales really needs her, she will fly out and defend the land. It will not be in my lifetime, nor in yours, Your Majesty, but when she is needed, she will be there!'

Everyone stared at Merlin, and then at the hole in the ground where the dragons had

The red dragon of Wales.

slept for so long. 'Now you can build your tower,' said Merlin. 'Nothing will disturb it.'

Without waiting for a reply, he turned and went away down the hill.

Merlin's red dragon is the dragon that we see on the flag of Wales. If you climb to the top of the hill where the two dragons slept, you will see a pool and the ruins of a tower. The hill is called Dinas Emrys.

Dinas Emrys is one of those places where the real world and the story world meet. In English, its name means Emrys' Fortress, or maybe Emrys' Castle. Who was Emrys? Go back to the beginning of this story and you will be reminded … and the names of places can remind us of the stories that happened there, long, long ago.

2

TWO GIANTS

Once upon a time, a long time ago, there were two huge friends. One was a giant called Idris, the other was a giantess called Bronwen. Bronwen lived in the hills called the Berwyns, near the river Dee, and Idris' home was on the coast, because he loved the sea.

They didn't see one another very often, because they lived far apart, and they missed each other. So one day Bronwen said, 'Let's each build a tower, so we can climb up and see each other and talk across the tops of the hills.'

Idris thought this was a really good idea, so they each chose a high place to build on.

They both made a good start on their towers, but the trouble was that they only had one hammer between the two of them. They had to share it by throwing it backwards and forwards. This worked well enough for a while, but soon Bronwen was getting on with her tower much faster than Idris. Idris was not happy about this, and began to get very grumpy.

'Hey! You're not sharing the hammer!' he shouted to Bronwen.

'Pardon? What did you say?' asked Bronwen.

'I said you're not sharing the hammer!' Idris repeated.

'Sorry, I can't hear you,' called Bronwen, bashing away, with an annoying smile on her lips.

'*I said I need the hammer!*' yelled Idris.

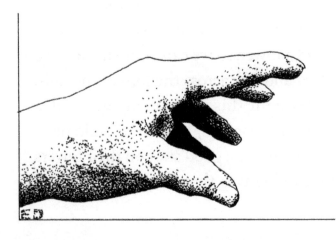

'*What?*' she yelled back.

'*I want the hammer!*' roared Idris.

'Aren't you going to say please?' asked Bronwen.

This was too much for Idris, and Bronwen could see this. She thought she had better throw him the hammer, after all. She knew what his temper was like. But just to be annoying, she threw it short. Idris, his face like thunder, had to plod down from his tower to look for the hammer. No sooner had he stomped back up to his building site, hammer in hand, than Bronwen was calling for it once more.

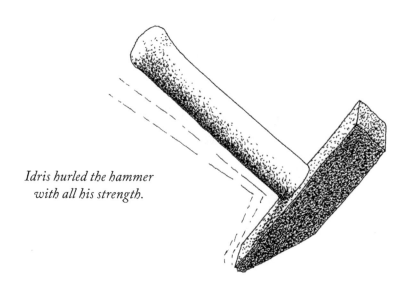

Idris hurled the hammer with all his strength.

She went on teasing and pestering him until he lost his temper completely.

'Keep the stupid hammer then!' he yelled at her, hurling the hammer with all his strength in a long high arc. It crossed the Berwyns, flew right over Bronwen's head, and disappeared behind her in the valley. It hit the ground with a great thump, leaving a big dent, which is still there today.

Without the hammer, neither of them could go on with their work. They went away and just left their half-finished towers. It wasn't long before the towers fell down. Two great rocky heaps are all that is left today.

The one in the Berwyns is called Cadair Bronwen, Bronwen's Chair. The other is the mountain Cadair Idris, above Dolgellau. People say that Idris sometimes comes back to Cadair Idris to sit in his chair, right on the top. Then he takes out his telescope and studies the stars.

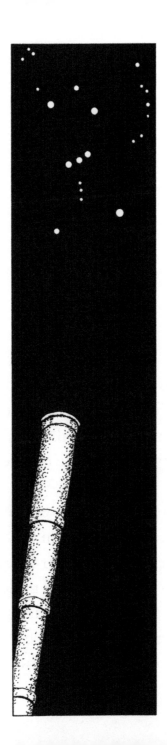

*Idris studies
the stars.*

3

THREE TASKS

Once upon a time there was a boy called Gareth who lived in a little village called Betws Gwerful Goch. He was an ordinary boy, and it was an ordinary village … except for the wicked wizard's castle on the other side of the river.

The wizard had captured many people, from near and far, even from Gareth's village, and he made them work for him. Whatever he told them to do, they had to do it.

One day, poor Gareth was captured too. The wizard made him work hard every day. He hardly got any food, and he had to sleep in a cupboard under the stairs. But the worst thing was that Gareth was lonely. He missed his friends, he missed his brother and sister, and most of all he missed his mum and dad.

He was so lonely that he used to talk to himself, because there was no one else to talk to. And that was how it all started …

One day, Gareth was working in the wizard's garden. He felt so sad that he gave a big sigh, and said, 'Oh, will I never get away from here?'

The wizard was in the garden, and he heard Gareth. He jumped out from behind a tree and gave Gareth a big fright. 'So,' he shouted, 'you want to leave us, do you? Well, I'm in a good mood today, so I'll make a bargain with you. I'll give you a task to do, and if you can do it before the sun sets, you can go free. But it won't be easy for you to do it. Come with me …'

The wizard led Gareth out of the garden and across a field to a small hill. The hill was covered in trees.

'I need some firewood,' said the wizard. 'Cut down all these trees – every one – and saw them into pieces for me to burn. If you can do it before the sun sets, you can go free. But it won't be easy for you to do it!'

The wizard laughed a wicked wizard laugh and went away, leaving Gareth staring at the hill. There were hundreds of trees: oak trees, ash trees, beech trees, birch trees, holly trees, rowan trees, larch trees, lime trees …

Gareth knew it would take him weeks to cut down all these trees. And he only had one day! It seemed hopeless. But however bad things are, however impossible something seems, if you don't try, you'll never know if you can do it or not.

So Gareth took a deep breath, picked up his trusty, rusty saw and carried it up to the top of the hill. There, he started sawing. And sawing. And sawing.

By the time the sun was high in the sky, he had only cut down two small trees, and there were still hundreds left. He stopped to rest. And saw someone coming up the hill. It was the wizard's youngest daughter, Tegwedd. She had noticed Gareth before, and had seen that he was a good little worker who tried hard to do his best. So she had decided to help him.

'Hallo Gareth,' she said. 'You've been working hard and you look very hot and tired. I've brought you a picnic. Come and sit down in the shade and have something to eat. It'll give you strength.'

Gareth was glad to put down his saw and have a rest. Tegwedd took the picnic out of her basket and laid it out. But before she sat down with Gareth, she took something else out of the basket. It was a silver-coloured cloth. She rubbed it gently over Gareth's saw, where he had left it on the ground. Then she sat down. As soon as the silver cloth touched it, the saw jumped up and started cutting down the trees and sawing them up … all by itself!

It worked so quickly that, by the time Gareth and Tegwedd had finished the picnic, the top of the hill was as bald as an egg, and every single tree had been cut into small pieces.

Gareth was amazed – but not too amazed to remember to thank Tegwedd for her help.

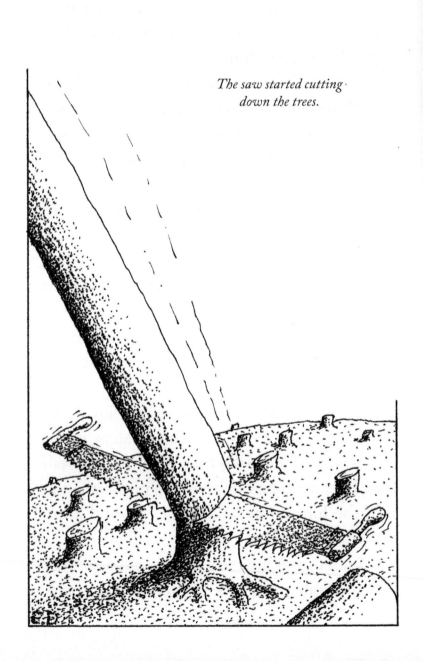

The saw started cutting down the trees.

'You're welcome,' she said with a little smile, and she put the picnic things and the silver cloth in her basket, waved goodbye and went away down the hill.

As Tegwedd was going down one side of the hill, the wizard was coming up the other. He wasn't glad when he saw all the firewood – he was mad!

He said, 'You couldn't have done all this work by yourself. Someone must have helped you. So I won't set you free. Instead, I'm going to give you another task. If you can do it tomorrow before the sun sets, you can go free. But it won't be easy for you to do it. Come with me!'

The wizard led Gareth down the bald hill and across the fields, until they came to the very edge of his land, where there was a rushing river. On the other side of the river was a cliff, going straight up into the clouds.

The wizard pointed at the cliff. 'At the top of that cliff, a great big bird has its nest. In the nest is a golden egg. If you can bring me that egg before the sun sets tomorrow, you can go free. But it won't be easy for you to do it!'

The wizard laughed his wicked wizard laugh and went away, leaving Gareth staring at the cliff. It was smooth and steep, and he couldn't see any way to climb it. He couldn't see any way to get across the water, either. There were no bridges or boats, and the river was too wide to jump across, too deep to wade across and too fast to swim across.

He sighed, and thought, 'This is hopeless.' But then he remembered how Tegwedd had helped him with the first task, and he had hope in his heart once more.

'She helped me today. Perhaps she will help me tomorrow,' he thought, and he went off to the cupboard under the stairs, to get a good night's sleep.

Early the next morning, Gareth was back on the riverbank, walking up and down, trying to find a safe place to cross. It seemed impossible.

Then he saw someone walking along the riverbank towards him. It was Tegwedd.

She came close and smiled at him. Then she bent down and took off her shoe. She held it up, and said to Gareth, 'Wish that my shoe was a boat.' So he did.

In the twinkle of an eye it became a little boat, just big enough for two, bobbing in the water.

Gareth and Tegwedd jumped in and easily rowed across the river. But when they climbed out on the other side, the cliff stretched up right in front of their noses. Smooth and steep, without a single handhold, it looked quite impossible to climb.

But Tegwedd smiled at Gareth. She held up her hand and said to him, 'Wish that my fingers were a ladder.' So he did.

In the twinkle of an eye, her fingers stretched up and up, until there was a ladder of skin and bone reaching up through the clouds towards the very top of the cliff.

Tegwedd said, 'When you get to the top of the cliff, you must be careful of the bird. It's always hungry. Take this piece of meat with you, and when you see the bird, throw the meat as far as you can. The bird will fly after the meat. You must find the golden egg in the nest and climb down before the bird comes back.'

She gave him a lump of meat. Gareth stuffed it into his pocket and thanked her. Then he began to climb the finger ladder.

Up and up and up he went. He climbed through the clouds. At last he could see the top of the cliff above him, with sticks and twigs from the untidy nest poking out over the edge.

Suddenly there was something else poking out too. A huge yellow beak like a pair of giant scissors was opening and shutting over his head, and two enormous round orange eyes were glaring at him. It was the biggest bird he had ever seen!

Gareth knew it could gobble him up in one gulp, and he was afraid, but he remembered the meat that Tegwedd had given him. He pulled it out of his pocket and threw it as far as he could.

The bird looked at the boy. It looked at the meat. Which one would it eat? Luckily, it chose the meat! Opening its huge wings, it swooped down and away. Its wings made so much wind that Gareth thought he would be blown away.

He held on tight to the ladder while it rocked in the wind. He felt it bend under his weight, and he thought he would fall. But he didn't. The ladder bent, but it didn't break.

When the air was calm once more, Gareth reached up and put his hand in the nest. He felt scratchy twigs. He felt soft moss. And then he felt the cool curve of a giant egg. He lifted it up. It sparkled and shone. It was the golden egg. He carefully put it into his pocket and began to climb down, before the great bird came back.

Down and down and down he went, until at last he was standing next to Tegwedd once more. He showed her the golden egg.

She smiled at him and said, 'Wish that the ladder was my fingers again.'

So he did, and her hand looked just the way it had before … at first. Then, Gareth saw that her little finger was a bit crooked, and he remembered how the ladder had bent when he leaned on it in the wind.

'Oh, I've hurt you!' he said. 'I'm sorry.'

'Don't worry, it's fine,' said Tegwedd. 'Now, come on, we must go back across the river.'

So they got into their little boat and crossed the river once more. When they were standing on the other bank, Tegwedd smiled and said, 'Wish that the boat was my shoe again.'

So he did.

Tegwedd took her shoe out of the water, shook out a few drops, and put it on. She smiled at Gareth once more and walked away.

As Tegwedd went away in one direction, the wizard was coming from the other. When he saw Gareth on the wrong side of the river, and no sign that he had been across, he was glad. But when Gareth showed him the egg, he was mad!

'You couldn't have got the egg by yourself,' he said. 'Someone must have helped you. So I won't set you free. Instead, I'm going to give you another task, and this time, no one will be able to help you, because I'll be there to watch you. Meet me tomorrow morning by the castle wall. If you can do the task I give you, you can go free. But it won't be easy for you to do it!'

The wizard laughed his wicked wizard laugh and went away.

Gareth sighed and thought, 'This is hopeless. How can Tegwedd help me this time? It's impossible.' He went off to the cupboard under the stairs, but he couldn't sleep. All night long he was worrying.

In the morning he went to meet the wizard. What else could he do?

The wizard was standing under the high wall of the castle. He laughed his wicked wizard laugh when he saw Gareth coming, and pointed up to the top of the castle wall.

'I have three daughters,' he told Gareth. 'I have changed them into three seagulls. If you can tell which one is Tegwedd, my youngest daughter, you can go free. But it won't be easy for you to do it!'

Gareth looked up and saw three seagulls perched on the wall. When the wizard snapped his fingers, they all flew down, and landed in a line on the grass in front of Gareth.

'Well,' said the wizard, 'which one is Tegwedd?'

Gareth looked at the first seagull. He looked at the second seagull. He looked at the third seagull. They all looked exactly the same. He sighed. He didn't know what to say. He was going to be the wizard's prisoner for ever.

Then one of the seagulls moved its foot. Only a tiny bit, but Gareth saw, and it made him look at the bird more carefully. He saw that it had pushed one foot in front of the other. He saw that the smallest claw on its foot was a bit crooked. Then he remembered how Tegwedd's finger had been bent when he leaned on the ladder.

'That one!' he shouted, pointing at the bird with the crooked claw. 'That one is Tegwedd!'

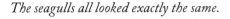

The seagulls all looked exactly the same.

Of course, he was right. The wizard did not laugh this time. He knew that his magic was broken. The three birds changed back into three girls, and the one Gareth had chosen was Tegwedd.

The wizard was so angry that he shook his fist and stamped his foot. When he stamped, a great hole opened in the ground under him and he fell down, down, down.

He was never seen again. Were they sad? No, they were glad. Now all his prisoners were free and they could go back to their own homes.

Gareth went home to his own village. Tegwedd went with him. Whenever Gareth needed help, Tegwedd was always there to help him. They lived happily ever after.

4

THREE WISHES

There was once a beautiful princess who didn't like being a princess. Her name was Dwynwen and she was one of twenty-four sisters. Their father was Prince Brychan and they lived on the lovely island of Anglesey.

Dwynwen didn't enjoy feasts and hunting and fine clothes: the thing she really liked was the beauty of nature, and she loved saying prayers and praising God. She wanted to be a hermit and find a quiet place to live all alone near the sea.

But Dwynwen's father didn't like this idea at all. He wanted her to marry someone grand, someone with land and money and power, so that their family would become even more important.

One day, he said to her, 'Dwynwen, it's time you got married. I've found you a nice boy. He's very rich. His name is Maelon. I think you are going to like him.'

But Dwynwen didn't like him. Well, she didn't mind him, he was quite nice, but she didn't want to marry him. She didn't want to marry anyone at all.

She told her father, 'I don't want to get married. I want to be a hermit and live quietly by the sea.'

He didn't like that.

He said, 'You should do what I tell you. I know what is best for you.'

But Dwynwen didn't think so. She ran away. She ran and she ran until she was so tired that she lay down under an old oak tree, and she fell asleep.

In her sleep she had a dream. She dreamed that an angel came to her with a sweet drink.

'Drink this, Dwynwen,' said the angel in the dream, 'and you will forget all about Maelon and be able to live peacefully here near the sea. In fact, after you drink this, Maelon will never trouble you again. God will change him into a block of ice.'

In her dream, Dwynwen took the cup from the angel and drank it down to the last drop. Soon afterwards, she woke up. But she hadn't forgotten Maelon. Instead, she felt really sad that he had been changed into a block of ice.

She thought, 'I shouldn't have let that happen. None of this is his fault.'

She worried and worried about Maelon. Then she saw the angel from her dream. Only this time, she was awake. The angel came up to her and smiled.

'Dwynwen,' said the angel, 'you haven't forgotten Maelon. Why do you keep thinking about him?'

'I shouldn't have let him be changed into a block of ice. It isn't fair. Please can you change him back?' she asked.

The angel smiled. 'If you really want that to happen, Dwynwen, you can do it yourself. I have come back to give you three wishes. You only have three, but whatever you wish for will come true. Choose your wishes well.'

'Oh, I will! Thank you,' said Dwynwen.

Then just as suddenly as she had appeared, the angel disappeared. Dwynwen was alone again. But she knew she had a chance now, with her wishes, to make everything all right.

She thought carefully for a minute or two, then she spoke.

'I wish that Maelon be changed back from a block of ice into a man,' she said. 'That is my first wish.

'I wish that I will never have to get married. That is my second wish.

'And I wish that God will let me look after all the people who are truly in love, and make their wishes come true. That is my last wish.'

Dwynwen's wishes all came true.

Maelon was changed back from a block of ice.

Dwynwen lived quietly by the seashore of Anglesey for the rest of her life, and the place where she lived was named Llanddwyn after her. She built a little church there, with a well for fresh water.

People who are in love still go to Llanddwyn to see the church and to look for Dwynwen's well.

They say that there is a magic fish in the well. If you see it swimming around inside the well, it means that Dwynwen has heard your wish to live happily ever after. And she will make your wish come true.

There is a magic fish in the well.

5

THE OLDEST ANIMALS IN THE WORLD

Once upon a time there was an Eagle who was very old and very lonely. His wife had died long ago and his chicks had all grown up and left the nest.

In the sadness of his heart, he thought it would help to get married again, but he didn't want to marry a young bird who would make him feel old and tired. He wanted to find a bird who was old. Really old, like him, so that the two of them could sit together quietly and keep each other company.

He had heard of an old Owl living in Cwm Cowlyd, and he thought perhaps she would be a good bird to ask.

'But is she as old as me?' he wondered. 'I don't want to marry a young bird …'

It didn't seem very polite to ask the Owl how old she was, so the Eagle thought he would ask a friend about her.

'I'll ask the Stag,' he thought to himself. 'He's older than me. He will know if the Owl is old.'

So the Eagle went to see his friend, the Stag of Rhedynfre, and asked, 'Do you know if the Owl of Cwm Cowlyd is old?'

'Hmmm,' said the Stag. 'I am old. Can you see this tree stump by me? I can remember when it was just an acorn at the top of a tree. I can remember when it fell down and started to grow. It took three hundred years to grow. For three hundred more years it was a tall and strong tree, and then it took another three hundred years to die. All that is left now is this stump, with no leaves and no branches. I have been here all that time, and I am old,

and the Owl of Cwm Cowlyd was already old
when I first met her. But I do have a friend
who is older than me. Perhaps she will know.
She is the Salmon of Llyn Llifon.'

So the Eagle went to see the Stag's friend,
the Salmon of Llyn Llifon, and asked, 'Do
you know if the Owl of Cwm Cowlyd is old?'

'Hmmm,' said the Salmon. 'I am old.
I have lived as many years as there are scales

The Stag of Rhedynfre.

on my body and as many years as there are eggs in my belly. I have been here all that time, and I am old, and the Owl of Cwm Cowlyd was already old when I first met her. But I do have a friend who is older than me. Perhaps he will know. He is the Blackbird of Cilgwri.'

So the Eagle went to see the Salmon's friend, the Blackbird of Cilgwri, and asked, 'Do you know if the Owl of Cwm Cowlyd is old?'

'Hmmm,' said the Blackbird. 'I am old. Can you see this stone next to me? I can remember when it was so big that you would have needed three hundred oxen to move it, and now it is as small as a nut. All that has happened to wear it away is that every night I wipe my beak on it before I go to sleep, and every morning I tap it with my wing when I wake up. I have been here all that time, and I am old, and the Owl of Cwm Cowlyd was already old when I first met her. But I do have a friend who is older than me. Perhaps he will know. He is the Toad of Cors Fochno.'

So the Eagle went to see the Blackbird's friend, the Toad of Cors Fochno, and asked, 'Do you know if the Owl of Cwm Cowlyd is old?'

'Hmmm,' said the Toad. 'I am old. I never eat any food except dust, and I only take tiny mouthfuls in case I use it all up. When I came here this flat place was a hill, like the high hills all around; but I have eaten it all up, and now it is a bog, though I only have a small appetite. When I first came here the Owl was already old, and she used to frighten me with her "to-whit-to-whoo", because I was only young. The Owl of Cwm Cowlyd is really, really old.'

Then the Eagle knew that the Owl of Cwm Cowlyd was older than him. In fact, she was the oldest animal in the world. And he knew he could ask her to marry him without being afraid that she would make him feel old and tired. The two of them would be able to sit together quietly and keep each other company.

So the Eagle went to see the Owl of Cwm Cowlyd.

'Dear Owl,' he said. 'Please will you marry me?'

'Oh!' said the Owl of Cwm Cowlyd. She was very surprised. But then she said, 'Yes.'

So they were married.

The Stag, the Salmon, the Blackbird and the Toad all came to the wedding. But nobody danced. They were all too old. They just sat together quietly and kept each other company.

After the wedding, the Eagle and the Owl lived together for a long time, and neither of them was lonely any more.

The Eagle asked the Owl to marry him.

6

HEN WEN THE PIG

Coll had a pig. He had lots of pigs, actually. Looking after them was his job. He lived in Cornwall with his pigs. He liked all his pigs and they liked him. But he definitely had a favourite pig.

Her name was Hen Wen. It means the Old White One. She was old. And white. And big – very big. Coll looked at her big belly, and he could see that soon she was going to give birth. He was looking forward to seeing Hen Wen's piglets.

The trouble was that a wizard had been to visit King Arthur.

The wizard could see the future. He said, 'An island of Britain will have terrible trouble, because of one of Hen Wen's babies.'

Arthur brought his knights to hunt Hen Wen, to kill her before her piglets were born.

Coll was horrified when he heard that King Arthur wanted to kill his favourite pig.

'Why?' he asked. 'She isn't causing any trouble. She's just a pig! Why doesn't the king like her? She's lovely …'

Hen Wen didn't wait for Arthur and his knights.

She ran down to the seashore. Coll ran down after her.

Hen Wen began to swim.

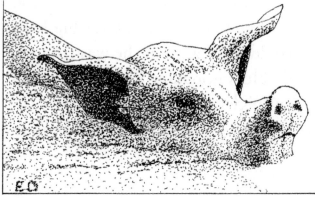

Hen Wen jumped into the sea. Coll jumped in after her.

Hen Wen began to swim. Coll held on tight to her tail, so that as she swam, she pulled him along.

Hen Wen swam right across the Severn Sea, from Cornwall to Wales. She escaped from King Arthur and his knights.

She came ashore in Gwent. She shook her head to get the water out of her ears, and a grain of wheat and a bee fell out of her right ear. Because of Hen Wen, Gwent become famous for wheat and honey.

Then she went back into the sea. She took Coll with her. She swam right along the south coast of Wales until she came to Pembroke.

She came ashore in Pembroke. She shook her head to get the water out of her ears, and a grain of barley and a bee fell out of her left ear. Because of Hen Wen, Pembroke became famous for its honeyed barley beer.

She went back into the sea again. She took Coll with her. She swam all along the west coast of Wales until she came to Snowdonia.

She came ashore and gave birth to a wolf cub and an eagle chick.

Coll was worried about these unusual babies. He remembered what the wizard had said. They didn't seem like the right sort of babies for a pig. He gave the eagle chick to The Man of the North. He gave the wolf cub to The Man of the West. He hoped they would be able to stop the strange babies from causing trouble.

Hen Wen went back into the sea with Coll. She swam along the Menai Straits and came ashore in Arfon, at the Black Stone. There she gave birth to a kitten!

Now Coll was really worried.

He said to himself, 'A pig isn't the right sort of mother for a wolf, or an eagle, or a cat!'

He looked at the kitten. It was the biggest kitten he had ever seen. It had been born with its eyes open and a mouthful of sharp teeth. It didn't look friendly. It looked like trouble. Terrible trouble.

Coll made up his mind. He didn't want to do it, but he knew he must. He picked up the kitten, turned round, and threw it into the sea. Hen Wen stared at him. There were tears in her eyes.

'I'm sorry, old friend,' said Coll. 'I feel like crying too. But I think that kitten would have made big trouble for us. Come on, let's go home. You should have little pink piglets to look after, not wild animals.'

Coll and Hen Wen swam back to Cornwall. What they didn't know was that the kitten was a good swimmer too. It swam right across the Menai Straits to the island of Anglesey.

The great big kitten came ashore in Anglesey. A man called Palug was walking along the beach. He saw it lying on the rocks, with its fur all dripping wet.

'You poor thing,' he said. 'You nearly drowned. I'll take you home and look after you.'

Palug took the cat home and his sons took care of the cat. They fed it well. It grew and grew and grew. Soon it was as big as a tiger, and just as fierce. People started to feel afraid of it. They called it Palug's Cat.

Silverweed, or Palf y Gath Palug.

It got really dangerous and started to attack people. Warriors tried to stop it, but it killed them one by one.

Palug sent a messenger to King Arthur.

'We need help!' said the messenger. 'Palug's Cat has killed ninety warriors. Please send a knight to save us.'

Arthur sent Sir Cai to save the people of Anglesey from Palug's Cat. The knight and the cat fought for a long time. The cat smashed Cai's shield to splinters. But Cai did not give up. At last he defeated Palug's Cat. Anglesey was safe.

The wizard had been right. One of Hen Wen's babies did cause terrible trouble to an island.

Palug's Cat is still remembered today. There is a plant with silvery green leaves and bright yellow flowers. It is called 'Silverweed' in English, and 'Palf y Gath Palug' in Welsh. This means 'Palug's Cat's Paw.'

I wonder why such a terrible animal had such a beautiful flower named after it. Maybe Palug's Cat wasn't quite as terrible as the wizard thought. Maybe it had a good side too. I like to think so.

7

THE AFANC

Seren lived near the river Llugwy. Her mother loved to sing, and Seren had a sweet voice too. Her father was a blacksmith, and Seren grew up to the sound of her mother's songs, the ringing of her father's hammer on the anvil and the crackle of the fire in the forge.

In those days, Betws-y-Coed was just a small village, and everyone relied on the river Llugwy for water and for food. There were plenty of fish in the river when Seren was a baby, but as she grew up, things changed. There were less and less fish in the river for the village people to eat. Something else was eating them. Nobody knew what this new creature in the river was, until it had finished all the fish, and started looking for something else to eat.

When it crawled out of the river, everyone was amazed by its huge size.

Then they were horrified, because it struck out with huge claws at the people who were standing near.

And then they were terrified, because it dragged two people back into the water to drown them and eat them.

This monster was an afanc, with sharp teeth and long claws, thick fur and a broad flat tail. Now, afanc is the Welsh word for 'beaver', and these days, beavers are small busy animals which build dams and only eat plants. But this afanc was a monster: as high as a house and as long as a ladder. And once it had decided it liked the taste of humans, life became a nightmare for the people living near the river.

Everyone was afraid of being taken by the afanc, and soon everyone knew someone who *had* been taken by the afanc, and never seen again.

Seren's parents stopped letting her go to the riverbank, even with friends, because, they said, no one would be able to save her if the afanc got near enough to take her.

A cold feeling of fear was everywhere.

One day, Seren's mother said, 'We can't go on like this! We don't feel safe in our own place. We need help.'

Seren's father agreed. 'You're right, my love,' he said. 'But who would be brave enough and clever enough and strong enough to get rid of this monster?'

Seren's mother had been thinking about this for a while.

'We need Hu Gadarn,' she said. 'He will know what to do.'

'Hu Gadarn! Of course! If anyone can help us, it will be Hu,' said Seren's father excitedly. 'That's the first good idea anyone has had since this trouble started.'

Soon Seren's mother's idea was being talked about all around the village.

And soon after that, a messenger was sent to find Hu and ask for his help.

Hu Gadarn had come over the sea to bring the first people to Wales, and he was wise and brave and strong. In fact, his name means 'Hu the Mighty'. When he heard about the troubles in Betws-y-Coed, he came at once to help.

He brought his two horned oxen with him. They were so big that their horns stretched right across the valley from one side to the other.

Everyone looked at the oxen in surprise. They already had one giant creature … why had Hu brought two more?

Then Hu explained, 'My plan is to drag the afanc away from here. Only my oxen are big enough to do that. And only the strongest iron chains will hold the monster. I need all you blacksmiths to make strong chains from your very best iron. Then they must all be joined together to make one long chain. We'll have to wrap it round the afanc as many times as we can to keep it from escaping. Then the oxen will pull it far away, so it can't cause any more harm.'

When they heard this, the blacksmiths looked at each other.

Seren's father spoke for them all, 'We can do it! We'll start today!'

Soon all the fires in all the forges of all the blacksmiths were blazing brightly. The whole valley rang to the sound of their hammers beating out hot iron. They shaped rings and linked the rings together.

When the blacksmiths had used up all their iron, they came clanking and clinking, carrying their chains, down the steep paths to the village. Seren's father was waiting, ready to forge the chains together into one mighty length.

But while the men were busy, Seren's mother was sitting quietly, watching the river in the distance, and thinking. At last, she went to find Hu.

'I understand your plan and it seems like a good one. But how will you get the afanc to come out of the water, and how can you make it wait while you chain it up?'

Hu Gadarn looked at her.

'That is the most difficult and dangerous part of this whole plan,' he said. 'We need to trick the afanc to come out of the water and settle down peacefully. I believe that if someone sits by the river and sings, the afanc will come out to listen. I think the music will calm it, so it will not attack the singer, but I don't know for sure. It's a very dangerous thing to ask someone to do.'

'It certainly is!' said Seren's mother, and she walked away with her forehead creased in a worried frown.

Hu Gadarn turned round in surprise when Seren suddenly appeared beside him. 'I heard what you told my mother,' she said. 'I'm a good singer. I will sing to the afanc on the beach.'

Hu looked at her. She was very young. He opened his mouth to tell her it was much too dangerous, but Seren spoke first, with a determined look on her face and her head held up high.

'I'm not scared,' she said. 'Well, yes, I *am* scared, but I know it has to be done and I think I would be a good person to do it!'

Hu stared at her. He changed his mind about what he was going to say.

'Do you know,' he said slowly, 'I think you might be right. But I don't think your mother will agree …'

Seren's mother said 'No'. She said, 'No, no, no!' She told Seren's father to say 'No' too.

But Seren argued with her. 'I *want* to do it. I want to help the village. Everyone says my singing is beautiful. Now here's a chance to make it useful as well!'

Of course, Seren's mother didn't want her to do it. Every mother wants to protect her children. But while they argued, the monster caught and killed three more people. One of them was a little boy who was only four years old.

His mother ran along the riverbank crying. 'Can't someone stop this beast before it kills all our children?' she wailed.

Seren looked at her mother. Seren's mother looked at the ground.

'If anything happens to you I will never forgive myself,' she whispered, and now it was her turn to cry.

Seren went to find Hu. 'What do I need to do?' she asked.

Hu's plan was simple, but he did not know if it would work. He would wait just out of sight, with the horned oxen, the end of the chain looped over their massive shoulders. All the blacksmiths would hide along the riverbank, holding the rest of the long chain ready in their arms, while Seren sat on the beach and sang.

If the afanc heard her, and *if* it liked her song, and *if* it came quietly out of the water, and *if* Seren could persuade it to lie down with its head in her lap, and *if* it went to sleep, the men would rush out and chain it up. Then Hu would get his oxen to pull it far, far away, to somewhere it would not cause any more trouble.

Everyone could see that there were a lot of '*if*s' in Hu's plan …

But they trusted him, so they were ready to try it.

Seren sat on the beach and looked at the river. She had known it all her life. But now it was no longer safe for her and her friends. She wanted to change that. She was afraid, but she was firm.

She looked around. Her father, holding the long chain, was hiding in the trees. He was the nearest person to her. He had insisted on that. He nodded to her. She nodded back. Everyone was ready; they were all in place.

Seren took a deep breath, and began to sing. At first her voice was wobbly, but soon she relaxed and she began to sing more clearly and strongly. Her voice drifted over the water. It must have penetrated the water, too, because, after a while, she saw bubbles rising in the middle of the river. Then she saw the huge sleek head of the afanc break the surface. It floated there, looking at her, and listening to her song.

Seren gulped with fear when she saw the afanc, but her song only stopped for a moment. She began again, singing about the deep blue water, the soft riverbed. The afanc listened, and swam closer to the shore.

Seren changed to a song about looking at the sky, lying in the sun. She didn't think the afanc could understand the words, but she wanted to do everything she could to make

The afanc swam closer to the shore.

it come out of the water, near enough for her father to catch it.

The monster was crawling up the beach.

She kept singing.

It was close enough for her to smell its wet, slimy coat.

She kept singing.

It was close enough for her to hear it puffing and panting.

She kept singing.

It was close enough for her to feel its breath on her face.

She kept singing.

Very, very slowly, as though it was hard work to move its giant body, it lay down next to her, and put its head in her lap.

Still singing, Seren began to stroke its head.

She changed the song to a lullaby.

She watched as the afanc's eyes began to close. She realised that her soft song was working: her lullaby was lulling the afanc to sleep.

She kept singing and stroking its head. But she lifted her other hand to signal to her father.

There was a long moment when nothing happened.

Then suddenly, the men were all around her. The chains were clashing together as they threw them over the monster, which was roaring and thrashing around. Her father grabbed Seren from behind and pulled her out from under the afanc. As he did so, it lashed out with its long sharp claws. Seren felt a horrible pain in her chest. She looked down and saw blood running down her dress. It was her own.

Her father carried her to the trees. Her mother ran to them, tore off her scarf and pressed it over the wound, to stop the bleeding.

They didn't take any notice of what was happening on the beach, where the men stood back from the afanc, wrapped in chains, and Hu Gadarn's oxen began to pull. Slowly, slowly the afanc was dragged up the beach, and the oxen drew it away.

The stories say that this was such hard work, even for the mighty horned oxen of Hu Gadarn, that they cried as they went over the top of the hills, and that the lake made from their tears is still there today.

The stories say that the oxen pulled the afanc all the way to Llyn Glaslyn in the shadow of Mount Snowdon, and that when they reached the edge of the lake the afanc jumped in, still with the chains around it, and Hu had to work fast to free the horned oxen before they were pulled in too.

The stories say that, even today, birds will not fly over the lake, in case the afanc leaps up and pulls them down.

But the stories do not say what happened to Seren after that day. I hope she was not badly wounded, and that the people of Betws-y-Coed still remember how brave she was.

8

ANOTHER DRAGON

Sir John was the Sheriff of Denbigh, and the great Castle of Denbigh was his home. It stands on a high rock above the town, with fabulous views in all directions.

But Sir John didn't spend much time at the castle – he didn't like puffing up the hill. It was hard work for him. He was very big, you see. In fact, he was as big as a giant.

And because the castle was nearly always empty, it was slowly falling down.

And because it was slowly falling down, a dragon took it over.

It made its home in the ruins of the castle, and it would fly out over the countryside, and come back with a sheep or a shepherd or a cow or a cowherd, to cook with its flames and eat for its lunch.

Soon the people of Denbigh were afraid for their lives.

'Who can save us?' they wailed.

Then the cry went up around the town, 'Sir John! Sir John!'

Hearing his name, Sir John came rushing to find out what had suddenly made him so popular. They told him about the dragon; they showed him the burns and claw-marks all around.

'Never fear! Sir John is here!' he cried. And he went away to put on his armour.

Now, a suit of armour big enough for a giant is not easy to find, and it's a shame that Sir John hadn't looked after it, because it would have been very useful for dragon slaying. Unfortunately, the suit was so old and rusty and stiff that Sir John could not move it, or even open the helmet.

'Never mind!' yelled this cheery hero. 'I'll see to him as I am!'

He picked up his sword, and set off up the hill to the castle to face the dragon. The good folk of Denbigh came out to cheer for him – but quite quietly, in case the dragon heard them.

Sir John went into the castle. There wasn't anyone there. Everyone had either run away from the dragon or been eaten by it.

If he was wondering how to find the dragon, he soon stopped. A huge, scaly, smoking head appeared around the Treasure House Tower, grinning horribly.

'How nice to have a visitor,' said the dragon. 'Now, do tell me, why have you come?'

'Dragon,' shouted Sir John, 'I have come to fight you. Get ready to die, for I have never been beaten in battle!'

'There's always a first time,' said the dragon, uncurling massively from where it lay under the Treasure House Tower, the Bishop's Tower and the Red Tower. It really was a very *big* dragon.

Blows crashed, claws clashed, stones tumbled, the earth rumbled. It was a bitter battle.

It really was a very big dragon.

Down below, in Castle Lane and Love Lane, in Lôn Parc, Lôn Ganol and Lôn y Post, the townsfolk shivered, prayed and crossed their fingers for luck.

Sir John needed a bit of luck. This dragon was a lot harder to fight than he had expected.

For the first time in his life, Sir John thought he was going to lose a battle. The dragon was larger than him, wasn't tired and was able to fly.

Sir John was fighting as well as he could, but he *was* tired, especially when the dragon started playing a trick, which it thought was very funny. It stood up on its hind legs, and biffed him flat on his face with one of its front claws. Then it swung its tail under him as he tried to get up, so that he flipped down onto his bottom. Sir John could see that this might be funny to watch, but it wasn't at all funny to be part of it.

The dragon was forcing him backwards towards the well. It was going to be a long way to fall. Sir John told himself it wouldn't do the dragon any good to push him down the well, because it would not be able to get him and eat him. But he knew that it wouldn't do him any good either …

Sir John realised that he was going to have to beat the dragon by being crafty, not strong. His brain started working as fast as his sword, as he tried to think of a way to trick the dragon before it finished him off. Then, as it reached up again to bash him on the back of the head, and he twisted round as far as he could to get out of its way, he saw a soft place under its wing, without any scales to protect it.

Hope filled his heart. He took two steps back, which put him right on the edge of the well, but just too far away for the dragon to reach. The dragon snorted and stretched, opening its wings to push itself forward. When it did this, he could see the soft skin under its wing.

Sir John stabbed suddenly with his sword, burying the blade in the dragon's side. With a terrible scream, the dragon fell – but then it got up again, looking really annoyed! Sir John was ready, and stabbed again. The dragon fell again. And got up again! Sir John stabbed a third time. This time the dragon fell and didn't move.

Sir John leaned on his sword until he had got his breath back, then he bent over and began to cut off the dragon's head. This might sound like a nasty thing to do, but he needed to be able to prove that the dragon was dead. If not, how was he going to get everybody to stop hiding and go back to normal life?

As he carried the horrid head down Castle Hill, the people of Denbigh came out once more to cheer him, and this time they didn't have to do it quietly!

9

TWO MORE GIANTS

The king of Ireland was out riding his horse one day. He galloped up a hill and looked down from the top at a large, lovely lake. It was called the Lake of the Cauldron, and as the king watched, the water in the lake began to boil and bubble, just like soup in a pot on the fire.

Then the king saw, or he thought he saw, red and yellow weed swirling around on the surface of the bubbling water. But it wasn't weed. It was hair!

Up from the water came the swirly stuff, and underneath this hair was a huge head, like a great round island covered in red and yellow grass, with water pouring off it as it came up.

Under the hair there were two enormous eyes.

Under the eyes there was a nose like a steep ski slope.

Under the nose there was a mouth like a wide wild valley.

Under the head there was a neck as massive as a mountain, and under the neck there was a huge body to match the huge head.

A giant appeared, sending great waves crashing as he walked. He waded out of the lake and shook the water out of his hair. He was carrying something on his back. It was a cauldron that matched his size. He seemed huge to the king, but when a woman followed him out of the lake, he looked quite small beside her. She was twice as big as he was!

The two giants looked around, and saw the king sitting on his horse at the top of the hill. They started to walk towards him. In only two steps, they had climbed the hill and were standing looking down at the king, who felt rather nervous as he looked up at them. But he didn't need to worry. The giants spoke to him politely.

'It is good to meet you,' they said, speaking together. 'Are you the king of this place above the water?'

'I am,' said the king, 'it is called Ireland. How are things going with you?'

'Well,' said the man giant, 'it's like this, Lord. My name is Llasar, and this is my wife Cymidei. In two months and two weeks, she is going to have a baby.'

'Yes,' said the woman giant, Cymidei, 'and the baby will be born with weapons in his hands, and he will already be a warrior and ready to fight whenever you need him.'

'Well,' said the king, 'I promise I will give you somewhere safe to stay until the baby is born.'

'Thank you,' said Llasar. 'In that case, we promise that you can use our cauldron whenever you need it.'

'Thanks to you too,' said the king with a smile. 'I'm sure that a cauldron as big as yours will be very useful for feasts at the palace. You must be able to cook soup for a hundred people in that!'

This is the Cauldron of Rebirth.

'No, Lord, you don't understand,' said Cymidei politely. 'This is not an ordinary cauldron. You can't use it for cooking. This is the Cauldron of Rebirth. It can bring dead warriors back to life.'

'What?' said the king in surprise. 'I have never heard of such a thing.'

'It is one of the Treasures of the Island of the Mighty,' said Cymidei. 'One day we will take it back there. It has been at the bottom of this lake with us for a long time. We are its Keepers.'

'We will let you use it if you need it. When a warrior is killed in battle, you can throw his body into the cauldron. In the night he will come back to life and next morning he will climb out again, ready to fight. No one who has been in the Cauldron of Rebirth is able to speak afterwards, because what they see there is secret, but they will be even better at fighting than they were before.'

'I see,' said the king. 'If we have a war, this cauldron will certainly help us to win. But there is no war in the land at the moment, I'm glad to say. Come back with me and I will find you somewhere to live.'

So the two giants, Llasar and Cymidei, followed the king to his palace and, true to his word, he found them a place to live nearby. They settled down, and after two months and two weeks a warrior baby was born. He was as fierce as could be!

Soon the warrior had a brother … and then another brother … and then another brother!

Every two and a half months, another warrior baby was born. They were all very quarrelsome. Soon they were fighting and causing trouble all over the land.

By the beginning of their second year in Ireland, Cymidei's children were causing so much trouble that people started to hate them.

By the time the second year was halfway through, people had had enough. They went to see the king.

'Lord,' they said. 'We had a peaceful life before these giants came. There was no war in our land. But they make too much trouble. You must get rid of them!'

The king was worried. He said, 'But I invited them here. They are my guests. What do you want me to do?'

'Get rid of them, or we'll get rid of you, and we'll choose another king!' shouted the people.

'I will ask my wise men what to do about them,' said the king sadly.

The wise men told the king, 'If you want to keep your crown, you must get rid of the giants. But it won't be easy. They will not go if you ask them. They like living here too much. And they won't go back in the lake again, that's for sure.'

'So what can I do?' asked the king.

One of the wise men had a terrible idea. He said, 'We will build a roundhouse made of iron, and invite Llasar and Cymidei and all the troublesome children to go inside for a feast.

'Then we will call all the blacksmiths, and the bronzesmiths, and the silversmiths, and even the goldsmiths. We will tell them to bring their hammers and their tongs and their bellows.

'We will put charcoal all round the outside of the iron house and then we will light a great fire. The smiths will blow on the fire with their bellows until the house is red-hot. Those troublesome giants will not come out of there alive.'

The king thought it sounded awful, but he could not think of anything else to do, and he did not want to lose his crown. So he agreed.

All the builders in the kingdom came. They built a roundhouse with iron walls and an iron roof.

All the cooks in the kingdom came. They cooked an enormous feast and put it in the roundhouse.

All the charcoal-burners in the kingdom came. They piled up baskets and buckets full of charcoal against the iron walls of the roundhouse.

Then the king invited Llasar and Cymidei and all their troublesome children to go inside. When they saw the feast, they sat down at once and started to eat and drink. The king quietly closed the iron door behind them. They didn't even notice, they were so busy eating …

Now all the smiths in the kingdom came. They locked the iron door with an iron key. They put iron chains all around the iron house.

They set fire to the charcoal and blew on the fire with their bellows until it was red-hot. The iron walls and roof began to glow red.

The smiths kept pumping their bellows to make the fire white-hot. The iron walls and roof began to glow white.

The king said, 'No one could live in that heat.' He turned and walked sadly away.

But Llasar, Cymidei and the children *were* all alive. They huddled in the middle of the roundhouse, as far from the white-hot walls as they could get.

'This is a trap,' said Cymidei.

'Yes,' said Llasar, 'they have locked us in, and soon the roof will fall.'

'What can we do?' asked Cymidei.

'If I'm quick, I can break through the wall,' said Llasar. 'You must follow me as closely as you can, and the children must follow you. It won't be easy, but we will all get out if you all do exactly as I say.'

Llasar looked around to check everyone was ready. He picked up the Cauldron of Rebirth and slung it on his back. 'If this is how the king treats us, we're not leaving the cauldron behind when we go,' he said grimly.

Then he ran at the wall. The iron in the heart of the fire was soft, and he easily broke through. Cymidei was right behind him.

But the quarrelsome children were not. They were arguing about who should go next. They pushed and shoved each other, shouting and yelling. They didn't follow their giant parents. And the next moment, the white-hot iron roof fell down on them. It was too late to get out.

The smiths shouted in dismay when they saw the two giants escape, but Llasar and Cymidei didn't stop. They ran and ran until they came to the seashore. Then at last they stopped, and looked out over the sea.

'What's on the other side of this sea?' asked Llasar.

'The Island of the Mighty,' answered Cymidei. 'The place where the Cauldron of Rebirth comes from. Let's take it back.'

Then she looked around. 'Where are the children?' she said.

But she already knew the answer. 'We've lost them all,' she said, and giant tears rolled down her cheeks.

Llasar put his arm around her. 'We can't stay here. We know we aren't welcome. Come on, it's time to go back underwater. We'll walk along the seabed until we come to the Island of the Mighty. Let's hope the people there will be kinder to us than the people here.'

Cymidei dried her eyes and nodded.

Hand in hand, without looking back at Ireland even once, the two giants waded out into the sea.

They walked until their heads were like two islands with waves breaking all around them.

They walked until their heads disappeared under the water, and their red and yellow hair swirled in the waves like seaweed.

They walked until they disappeared under the waves.

Along the seabed they walked, through seaweed forests with fish swimming through the branches like birds, going deeper and deeper, until they were in the very middle of the sea between Ireland and Britain. They kept walking until the sea got shallow again. They came out on the shore of Wales at Dinas Dinlle.

They looked around at the new land.

'What sort of welcome will we get here?' asked Cymidei.

'I think things will be different here,' said Llasar. 'The king of this land is a giant, like us. I think we will be welcome.'

He was right.

The king of the Island of the Mighty was Bran the Blessed, Bendigeidfran, who was so tall that there was no building anywhere in the land that was big enough for him. He was pleased to meet two more giants, and gave them a warm welcome.

When Cymidei told him that she would have a baby every two and a half months, he just smiled and said, 'We have plenty of room here in Wales. You and your children are all welcome.'

Those quarrelsome children spread out all over the land and lived in small groups, and that way they did not cause too much trouble. They protected the people where they lived, and they did a good job, because they were the best men with the best weapons that anyone had seen.

Llasar and Cymidei gave the Cauldron of Rebirth to King Bran, to thank him for making them feel at home. They told him how to use it.

'I hope I never have to use it,' he said. 'I hope there will never be a war.'

So Llasar and Cymidei, the Keepers of the Cauldron of Rebirth, lived happily in Wales for the rest of their lives.

10

DANCING WITH THE FAIRIES

Once upon a time, and it must have been a long time ago, there were two brothers who lived near Wrexham. They carried coal from Minera over the moor with their pony and cart, and this kept them very busy.

Usually they finished work before it grew dark, but when the long summer days came, they made as many journeys as they could. Sometimes they were still out on the moor as darkness fell.

One summer night they were on their way home to Minera. The empty cart was rattling behind their little pony, and the full moon made the night almost as bright as day, so that they could easily follow the path. They were both enjoying the peaceful night as they walked along beside the cart.

Then Dylan stopped, listened, and asked, 'Do you hear that, Dewi?'

They both listened. They could hear music somewhere on the moor. They turned off the track, leaving the pony. It put its head down and started to eat the grass at the side of the path.

The two boys came to the edge of a little dip in the moor, and peered over its side. To their astonishment, they saw a group of fairies dancing in a ring. They looked at the dancers, then at each other.

Dewi had horror in his eyes. 'The Fair Folk,' he whispered. 'We must get away!'

But Dylan had stars in his. 'Did you see her, Dewi, the girl with the long red hair? She looked at me. She smiled at me. She's lovely, isn't she? Watch, here she comes again!'

Dewi was even more worried now than before. 'Dylan, don't be daft now. Look away. Look away. Oh ... no ...'

He reached to grab his brother's arm, but it was too late. Dylan, his eyes on the fairy dancer, was holding out his hand to her. She grabbed his wrist and pulled him over the edge of the dip and into the dancing ring.

As soon as he was in the circle, the fairies made a spell of invisibility, and everyone, including Dylan, disappeared from sight.

'Oh no! Oh no! What shall I do? What shall I do?' muttered Dewi, running up and down helplessly on the edge of the dip. He did not dare to go down into it, because he was sure that the fairies were still there, even though he could not see them. If the fairies were still there, he thought, then Dylan must be too.

He knew it would not be easy to rescue Dylan. But he knew too, that unless his brother escaped before dawn, the fairies could keep him for ever, and he would be lost.

Dewi turned to look around the moonlit moor. He was looking for a tree. A rowan tree, which is the one tree that the fairies dare not touch. But he could not see any trees standing tall among the bracken and heather.

He looked around again. This time he saw their pony, standing on the path in the moonlight, with its nose down in the grass and the cart behind it.

The cart! Its wheels were made of rowan. As far as Dewi could see, it was the only rowan for miles around. He led out the pony from between the shafts, before throwing the little cart on its side, glad that it was empty and he did not have to tip out a load of coal.

Dewi only had until dawn to rescue Dylan. The fairies would dance all night, but once the sun rose, they would disappear, and he would never see Dylan again.

It was hard to get the wheel off the cart, but at last it was free. Dewi scrambled back to the edge of the dip.

He knew that what he really needed was a long branch from a rowan tree, and two strong men to help him hold it out into the space where the invisible fairies were dancing.

This would give Dylan a chance to grab the end of the branch, so that the rescuers could pull him out of the circle and break the spell. Then he would be visible once more.

Dewi was only one boy, and all he had was a wheel, not a strong branch. But it would have to do.

He got ready by pressing himself against a stone at the edge of the dip, so that he could not easily be pulled over. Then he leaned over the stone, holding out the wheel as far as his arms would reach.

'Dylan!' he shouted. 'Dylan, brother, catch hold here! I'll get you out. Trust me!'

A hissing, spitting noise came out of the air in reply. Dewi shivered, but he did not stop. He held out the wheel, and began to move it through the air, calling out his brother's name.

Suddenly, the wheel bumped against something: something that wasn't there, or, at least, could not be seen. Dewi almost fell, but recovered himself as he wobbled on the edge of the dip. He planted his feet, clutched the wheel with both hands and began to pull it towards him. He knew that his invisible brother, spinning in the fairies' dance, had bumped into the wheel and now was holding on to it as tight as he could.

Dewi pulled and pulled. He could feel the fairies dragging Dylan back, trying to keep him, but they could not touch the rowan wood. He knew that, as long as he could pull hard enough, their spell would be broken and Dylan would be free.

Suddenly Dewi fell on his back. The wheel thumped down on his chest and knocked his breath out of him. It was heavy, much heavier than it had been. He wheezed and gasped and puffed and panted. When he managed to open his eyes, he saw Dylan lying on top of the wheel. No wonder it was so heavy!

'You were right,' said Dylan. 'The fairies are dangerous. Oh, but that red-haired girl was lovely ...'

'Never you mind about that,' said Dewi sharply. 'Help me get the wheel back on the cart or we'll never get home. And you make sure you keep well away from the Fair Folk from now on, though what they see in you I really don't know.'

Dewi and Dylan came safely home.

And so the two brothers came safely home to Minera, just before the sun rose on another lovely summer day.

11

MAKING MUSIC FOR THE FAIRIES

Siôn Robert played the harp. He loved to make music for people to dance. Everybody said he was the best harper on the wide moor of Hiraethog, and when anyone had a Merry Evening they always asked Siôn to come to play. One night he was asked to make the music for Anwen's birthday party, down at Cefn Brith. He was looking forward to seeing old friends there, and he wrapped his harp carefully, put it on his shoulder and set out.

He crossed the moor in the sunlit afternoon and reached the hall just before it got dark. Siôn did all the walking, but the harp did all the talking; its music ringing out as it bumped on his back.

'Siôn, there you are! Welcome!' called Anwen's mother, coming over to him, her happy face all smiles. 'It's going to be a good night. Come and have a rest. The dancers won't be here for an hour.'

Siôn knew the time would fly by, and he was happy to sit in a corner and tune his harp while Anwen's family cleared a space for dancing. Lanterns were lit, tablecloths spread, plates of food put out.

Soon the room was full of people and it got warm. Siôn didn't mind. He loved to play. And this is why everyone always asked Siôn to make the music for parties. No one played as merrily as he did.

The evening really was a merry one, and the young ones danced late into the night. When at last the dancers went home, Anwen's mother thanked Siôn and paid him. He picked up his harp, ready for the journey home.

It was a long walk, but his head was full of tunes, and his feet knew the way without much help from his brain, so he was able to dream as he wandered on the moor, past the shining lake, which always reflected the moon.

But tonight the lake was different: it reflected hundreds of lanterns. Siôn stopped. Was he lost? No, he knew where he was, and he knew the lake. But there was a great palace next to it, all lit up. It should not be there. It had never been there before. But it *was* there! Siôn was confused, but he kept on walking.

As he passed the palace, a man in fine clothes called his name, and ran down the steps towards him.

By now Siôn was frightened, and if he hadn't been carrying his precious harp he might have run away. But the man spoke politely.

'Mr Siôn Robert! Sir, we are really glad to see you. Please, will you come in?'

He was so polite that Siôn decided to follow him up the marble steps. They went into a ballroom, full of fine folk enjoying a marvellous evening. The hall was very grand, with soft sofas, and tables covered with gold plates and dishes. The man offered Siôn a golden cup of wine, which he drank gratefully, for he was thirsty after his long walk.

A beautiful lady with a warm smile said, 'Siôn Robert, we are so pleased to see you here. We know your name and we know about your wonderful music, but we have never heard it. Will you play for us now?'

Siôn bowed to the lady and unwrapped the harp for the second time that night.

This was not the simple kind of Merry Evening that Siôn was used to, but he knew he would feel comfortable as soon as he had the strings of his harp under his fingers. The fine folk looked as bright as birds in their lovely clothes as they moved their heads and hands in time with the tunes. When he finished, they clapped and praised him for a long time. Then a merry man dressed in gold and brown took Siôn's hat and passed it round. Everyone put some money in, until the hat was full of sparkling gold coins. Siôn's tired eyes sparkled then too!

Leaving him to pack up his harp and his reward in peace, the guests went to the tables, and a meal was served. The servants made sure that Siôn had plenty to eat too. After the feast, the guests left one by one, until Siôn was alone. He was so tired after his long night that he did not want to think about walking home.

So he lay down on a velvet sofa, took the gold coins out of his hat and put them in his pockets, and made sure his harp was close by. Then he pulled his hat down over his face, and fell fast asleep.

He slept until the sun woke him up, shining through his hat into his eyes. The sun seemed very bright. Then he realised why. He wasn't indoors any more. He was lying on the ground beside the lake. The palace had gone. All the people in it had gone. Everything in it had gone!

Siôn jumped up in fright, wondering if his harp was still there. It was. He breathed a sigh of relief about that, picked it up and set off for home without looking back. He had the uncomfortable feeling that if he stayed there too long, the fairy magic would begin to work on him again.

He passed the lake many times more after that, but he never saw the wonderful palace again. And though he was always proud to think that the fairies liked his music, he didn't make any money from his time with them. Halfway home, he looked in his pockets, only to find that the gold coins of the fairies had all turned into brown leaves.

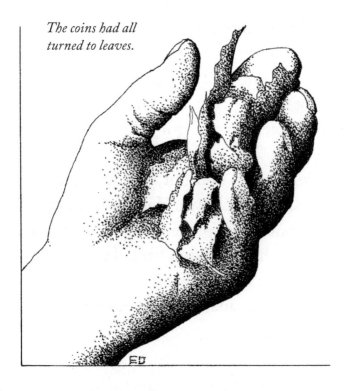

The coins had all turned to leaves.

12

SIX AND FOUR ARE TEN

Dic Spot the Cunning Man was born in 1710. His real name was Richard Morris, and he got his nickname because he had a big spot near his nose. Dic's Auntie Deborah was a fortune-teller, and she taught him to tell fortunes when he was only a teenager. He was so good that, before long, no-one wanted Auntie Deborah to tell their fortune any more: they all wanted Dic Spot.

Soon he was good enough to be called Dyn Hysbys, a Cunning Man, and he became famous all over North and Mid-Wales. He travelled around telling fortunes and making magic.

One day Dic Spot was on his way to Llanrwst in the Conwy valley. A farmer there wanted Dic to tell his fortune, to help him decide if buying some fields near the river Conwy was a good idea. Dic didn't have a horse. He was walking there. It was a long walk, and he was getting tired. He stopped at the inn in Henllan for something to eat, because he knew that he still had a long way to go.

Dic ordered beer, bread and cheese and he enjoyed his meal. He was very happy with his food, but when the bill came he was not so happy. The landlord wanted him to pay four pence for the beer and six pence for the bread and cheese! This was much, much more than the proper price, and Dic knew it. The greedy landlord thought it would be easy to cheat Dic because he was a stranger. But he was making a big mistake!

Dic paid the bill without saying a word but, before he left, he scribbled a few words on a scrap of paper, folded it very small and tucked it under the leg of the table. The landlord smiled at Dic as he left. Dic smiled back. He knew what would happen to the next person who went into that room, because the piece of paper had a spell on it.

As it happened, no-one else went into that room for the rest of the day. When it was getting late, the landlord and landlady went upstairs to bed, telling the sleepy maid to clean Dic's table before she finished for the night. She shuffled wearily into the room with a cloth in her hand, but as soon as her foot touched the floor of the room, Dic's spell started to work. She didn't mean to, she didn't want to, but she couldn't stop herself. She began to jump and hop around in a mad dance, all the while shouting out a song:

> Six and four are ten,
> Count it over again!

The landlord and landlady were upstairs in their bedroom. They could hardly believe their ears.

'What's got into that girl?' grumbled the landlord. 'Singing and dancing when good folk are trying to get some sleep! If she carries on, this is her last day working for us, and I won't pay her either.'

The landlord stomped downstairs in his nightshirt, ready to box the girl's ears. But as soon as he stepped into the room where she was dancing, the spell caught him too, and he began to leap about, shouting out the same tuneless tune as the maid:

> Six and four are ten,
> Count it over again!

His wife sat bolt upright in her bed when she heard the sound of their voices from downstairs. Her husband was dancing with the maid? In his nightshirt too? Her face and ears turned red with anger. She heaved out of bed, and stormed downstairs to give them both big trouble.

She went angrily into the room, but straightaway the spell caught her too, and she began to spin and dance, adding her voice to the song:

Six and four are ten,
Count it over again!

By now the noise could be heard from outside, and soon the neighbours were peeping round the front door wondering what on earth was going on. Seeing the landlord, his wife and their maid all bouncing about and yelling at the tops of their voices, they came in to complain about the noise. But, as soon as they were in the room, they began to whirl and twirl as well, adding their voices to the noisy song:

Six and Four are Ten,
Count it over again!

As the noise grew, so did the number of people being disturbed, and one after another, more and more people came in, only to find themselves bewitched and bounding, till the inn was full to bursting and the noise of the song was ear-splitting:

Six and four are ten,
Count it over again!

Who knows how long this might have gone on, or what would have happened next, if there had not been one bright spark among so many silly billies?

One young lad, a village boy called Aled, stood beside the open door and watched for a while. Seeing where and when his friends and neighbours started to dance, he understood that there must be a spell on the floor of the room. The landlord was too puffed out from dancing to tell him what had been happening there but, luckily, Aled had spent the evening leaning on a wall to watch people coming and going round the village, the way teenagers still like to do. He had seen Dic Spot leave the inn. He knew that Dic could cast spells.

'So that's what's going on,' thought Aled.

Without wasting any time, he took a horse from the stables and rode out of the village on the path to the west, up onto the moor. The inn was at a crossroad but, by luck, he chose the way that Dic Spot had taken. Soon enough his horse caught up with Dic, because he was only walking. Aled jumped down from his horse's back and began to tell Dic what was going on in Henllan. As he listened to the tale, a great big grin spread across Dic's face.

'Please, sir,' said Aled politely, 'please undo your spell. Please think of the danger all those people will be in if they keep dancing for days, with no food and no drink and no rest.'

Dic Spot thought for a moment, then slowly nodded his head. 'That landlord is greedy, and he needs to learn a lesson. But you are right: there are plenty of innocent people there. And you speak very politely. So I will listen to you. I will tell you how to undo my spell. Go back to the inn and find a piece of paper under the leg of one of the tables. I put it there, and it has my dancing spell written on it. Throw that paper into the fire. When it is gone, the spell will be too.'

Aled thanked him, and mounted his horse again.

'Wait!' called out Dic. 'Unless I put a spell on you to protect you, you will start dancing the minute you go into the room, and you won't be able to stop. Come here, young man.'

Dic whispered a spell into Aled's ear to protect him. Then he watched as the lad rode back to Henllan. Aled went as quickly as he could, eager to break the spell and save the tired villagers.

Sure enough, as soon he threw the tiny piece of paper into the fire, all those kicking legs and stamping feet were freed from the magic, and the song being shouted from all those sore throats was silent at last.

Six and four are ten,
Count it over again!

Aled was praised by everyone for saving them all. But nobody forgot Dic Spot the Cunning Man, and what he could do with his magic. And the greedy landlord treated strangers much better from that time on … which is what Dic Spot really wanted!

13

BELLA FAWR

Bella Fawr was the Witch of Denbigh. She was not the only witch in the town, and maybe she wasn't the biggest, in spite of her nickname, which means Big Bella, but she was the most popular!

Bella could undo bad spells that other witches had made. She helped people from near and far, though, of course, they did have to pay her. This is the story of how she helped John and Beti Griffiths.

John Griffiths had a farm called Ty Mawr. Not far away was the home of an old woman who made her living by begging from door to door. One day she came, as she often did, to the back door of Ty Mawr. Beti Griffiths opened it.

'Good morning to you, neighbour,' said the old woman, holding out a battered tin. 'Can you give me some milk to fill my little pot, please? I'm sure with fine cows like yours you can spare some milk for an old lady like me.'

But Beti was not having a good day. She had already hurt her thumb, broken a jug and had a row with John about the kitchen floor, because he had walked all over it with mud on his boots. She frowned at the old woman.

'No, I've none for you today, so off you go.'

The old woman stared at Beti, as if she couldn't believe her ears. She held out the tin again and shook it.

'You can see that it's empty,' she said. 'Are you going to send me away with nothing?'

'Yes, I am,' replied Beti crossly. 'I've told you, I've no milk to give you today, and too much to do. There's milk waiting to be turned into butter while you keep me here on the doorstep. Be off now.'

The old woman turned away, muttering. These were her words, too low for Beti to hear,

She churned the milk.

but loud enough to make a spell: 'Then the milk can wait for you and you for it.'

Beti shut the door on her and went down to the dairy. There she got busy, ready to make butter from the bowls of milk on the stone shelf. She poured the milk into the churn. Then she put in the churn dash to turn the milk round and round until it changed into butter.

She churned the milk. And churned. And churned. It did not change into butter. She kept going. Some days it took time to get the rhythm right. Some days the weather made things slow. But today it just did not happen at all. She worked until she was too tired to carry on. She rested a while, then started again. But the butter still would not come and the milk began to smell bad.

When John came in from the yard there was no cloth on the table, no food set out, no sign of Beti. He called her name, and when he got no reply he went from the kitchen down to the dairy. There sat Beti, red in the face, the churn dash in her hand and the dairy full of the bad smell of the milk.

'The butter won't come and the milk has turned bad, and I'm still angry with that old woman who came this morning,' she told him, nearly in tears.

At first John couldn't work out what she was talking about. But then he began to understand. Their neighbour, like many old women down the ages, did have a reputation as a witch.

'Did you turn your back to her? Or speak in a way that wasn't polite?' he asked.

Beti looked scared. 'I didn't give her milk. Why should I? She comes asking nearly every day. I was busy. I had such a lot to do … do you think she has put a spell on the milk?' she asked fearfully.

'The milk or the churn. We'll soon see.' John poured the bad milk away. Beti washed out the churn, then started again with fresh cream. But once again she could not get the butter to come. Instead the milk turned smelly and bad. They threw it away, for it was not even good enough for the pigs to eat. Beti began to cry.

But John was thinking. 'Beti,' he said, 'we'll ask Bella Fawr for help. I'll go tomorrow. She'll lift the spell. Don't worry.'

A witch to stop a witch: it made sense.

The next morning, John saddled his big brown horse and left early. In his saddlebag he had thick slices of ham wrapped in paper, a jar of honey, and a new pair of winter socks that Beti had made. He hoped these things would please Bella.

He also took a black hen in a covered basket, for this was the right thing to give to a white witch.

He worried all the way about whether Bella would really be able to help.

But Bella Fawr amazed him. She was large, fierce and not very clean, but she was as sharp as a knife. She put the hen out in her yard with a pleased nod, gave the basket back to John and told him to sit down at her kitchen table.

She stared at him for a while and then, much to his surprise, began to tell him all about his farm and even the names of his fields.

'Mistress Bella, you're right. About everything. But how … ?' John stopped himself from saying any more. It was not a good idea to ask witches to explain things.

Bella nodded slowly. 'Do not ask questions about my powers. The only thing you need to know is that I can help you. Listen carefully: you must do exactly as I say.'

'Yes, Mistress, of course,' John nodded. But Bella was not looking at him. She was looking into the distance. He was sure that, somehow, she was looking at his farm, even though it was half a day's ride away.

Then she said, 'You must put all your animals, every single one, into Gors Goch.'

Of course, John knew that this was the field in front of his house. A holly tree grew in the corner, which each year gave them branches covered with red berries to make the house bright with Christmas cheer. He did not expect her to know about the tree. But it seemed that nothing was hidden from her.

'When all your animals are in that field, you must go into the field at night, and hide behind the holly tree. Take someone else with you. Not a woman. This is woman's magic, and if another woman is there it will give the witch more power. At midnight she will come into the field, in pain from the spell I will put on her now. Do not let her see you are there, and watch what happens. She will lift her spell. It is the only way she can get free from mine.'

John nodded.

'I put this spell on her,' continued Bella, 'with this magic and with these words.'

She stood up, and began to speak in a loud deep voice. 'I put my spell on the witch who has put a spell on Beti Griffiths' milk. I put my spell on her evil magic and her evil heart. And I take all her magic away from John Griffiths' animals: his cows, and his calves, and his sheep, and his lambs, and his horses, his hens and his pigs, and all the creatures that he owns. I take off all spells and all trouble from every one of them.'

Then Bella sank down in her chair and didn't say anything more. She looked as though she was half asleep. She didn't even seem to notice when John got up, thanked her and left. But though making the magic spell had tired her out, it had worked.

A few days later, John took all his animals into Gors Goch. The cows were unhappy, and turned round and round, mooing loudly. All the other animals seemed calm, in spite of being so crowded together. His brother came to supper, and when it got late he went out with John to the field. They stood in the dark under the holly tree and waited.

After a long time, they heard the gate open, and someone came into the field, moving in pain. It was the old woman who had made the spell. She stood in the middle of the frightened animals, muttering in a low voice that John could just hear, though he could not make out the words. Then she coughed and spat. After that, she turned and went out of the field.

John and his brother looked at each other in the dark. They were both shivering, but not because they were cold.

'Look at the cows now,' said John's brother. The animals, which had been so nervous and worried, now stood there calm and quiet and peaceful.

The next day, when Beti went into the dairy, the butter churned easily and the milk stayed sweet. It was the same every day from then on. Bella Fawr had broken the spell. She really was a powerful witch!

14

THE PRINCE'S WIZARD

When Llywelyn the Great was our prince, that was a merry time in North Wales! With his beautiful wife, Siwan, a king's daughter, he ruled a happy, proud people. Their court in the Conwy valley was entertained by talented musicians, clever poets and brilliant storytellers.

One year near Christmas time, Llywelyn and Siwan opened a letter from Siwan's father, King John of England. It said, 'Come to my palace in London for the Christmas holiday. For twelve days and nights we will have the best of everything!'

Llywelyn and Siwan told their knights and soldiers and maids and dressmakers, 'Get ready to travel with us to London!'

When the prince and princess set out, it was a wonderful sight. Banners waved in the wind, horses stepped out proudly, the lords and ladies, soldiers and servants smiled and waved to the people who came out to cheer them on their way.

Their procession followed the river Conwy south, away from the sea. But just before they crossed the river at Llanrwst and turned to leave their dear Conwy valley, the prince and

They crossed the river at Llanrwst.

princess suddenly had to stop, because out in front of them jumped a strange little man.

He had long red hair and a long red beard. He wore a ragged brown tunic. His bare hairy legs and big dirty feet stuck out underneath.

Llywelyn's soldiers ran forward, in case this wild-looking man was dangerous. But the red-haired little man bowed low, and the prince said to his men, 'Wait! This is one of my people. He does not mean any harm. Let me hear what he wants to say.'

The red-haired little man looked at Llywelyn. He said, 'My Lord, you have many people with you, and you think you have everyone that you need. But you should take

me to London with you, too. Then, when you need my help, I will be there.'

The soldiers burst out laughing at the idea that their prince needed the help of a funny little man with no trousers!

But Llywelyn answered the way a prince should answer, 'Thank you my friend. I cannot really see how you can help, but since you offer to serve me, I gladly accept. But we have no horse for you. How will you travel with us to London?'

'Lord, do not worry. I will run beside you,' said the little man.

And to everyone's astonishment, he did. He ran all the way to London and never seemed tired or got left behind the riders. By the time they reached the king's palace, even the people who had laughed at him agreed that he was a very unusual man.

There was a warm welcome from Siwan's father, King John. There were good stables for the horses and comfortable rooms for the people. When they had all rested after their long journey, there was the first of the twelve Christmas feasts to enjoy.

Llywelyn and Siwan came into the Great Hall. It was bright with candlelight and loud with chatter. Long tables were set out in the hall and there was a place for everyone. At the High Table, Llywelyn and Siwan sat one on each side of King John. Soldiers, maids, friends and companions were shown to their places at the tables. Even the red-haired, bare-legged man was given a seat, near the kitchen boys.

Servants brought in food and drink: meat of the best and wine of the full glass. Everyone ate and drank until their plates were empty and their bellies were full. Then King John turned to his guests from Wales.

'Now,' he said, 'it is time for some entertainment.'

He gave a signal, and a man stepped into the space between the tables. He wore a robe covered with stars and a tall pointed hat. Everyone could see that he was a wizard, and an important one too. He was the King's Wizard of England.

He bowed to the king, and looked up at him as if to say, 'Shall I begin, Your Majesty?'

The king nodded. The wizard lifted his arm and moved it slowly through the air.

Suddenly, the space between the tables was filled with water, splashing gently against the tables, while fish leapt over the waves. A fleet of small ships sailed across, with tiny sailors steering the ships and setting the sails. Although the hall was full of water, no one had wet feet. They all laughed and clapped in amazement.

The wizard waved his arm, and ships, sails, fish and sea were all gone in the blink of an eye.

Then he moved his arm again. This time a farmyard appeared, with hens and ducks, sheep and goats and black and white cows. Milkmaids ran in with stools and buckets, and sat down to milk the cows. Then they gave fresh milk to the people sitting at the tables. It was delicious! When everyone had drunk, the wizard moved his arm again and everything he had made by magic disappeared.

There were cheers and shouts, and the wizard bowed low to King John, and then looked at him as if to ask, 'Did I do well, Your Majesty?'

The king smiled and nodded. 'Yes, you have done very well.'

The wizard bowed again and then, taking no notice of the shouts for more, he walked back into the shadows.

King John turned to Prince Llywelyn, 'Did you enjoy the magic?'

'Very much, Your Majesty,' said Llywelyn.

'Well, I have an idea. I am the host, and I will set out a fine dinner every night of the Christmas Feast. But we can take it in turns to provide the entertainment. My wizard pleased us all tonight. Why don't you arrange something just as good for tomorrow night, if you can? Do you agree?'

Llywelyn could hardly refuse. He decided to accept the king's challenge. He smiled and said, 'I agree, Your Majesty. Who knows, perhaps the Prince of Wales can show the King of England more magic than he has already.'

'Hmmm,' said King John, who was not very pleased with this idea. 'You speak bold words. We will see if you live up to them at tomorrow night's feast.'

Llywelyn bowed and left the king's table, a smile still on his face. But inside he did not feel like smiling. He did not have a royal wizard who could make magic. What was he going to do?

As he went out of the hall, someone came up to him. It was the red-haired, bare-legged little man.

'My Lord,' he said, bowing low, as he had done the first time Llywelyn saw him. 'You need my help, and I will not let you down. Let me be your wizard. You can trust me.'

Llywelyn could not believe that this ragged little man could help him. But he gave the kind of answer a prince should give, 'Thank you for your offer. I accept. Come to me tomorrow and I will give you a fine cloak to wear.'

'Oh, no, My Lord,' said the little man. 'I will make magic for you just as I am. I do not want different clothes.'

Llywelyn's heart sank as he looked at the little man's torn tunic, his bare feet and hairy legs.

Everyone in King John's fine court was going to laugh at this ragged little man. But

Llywelyn was a prince, and a prince must trust his people.

'Very well,' he said. 'I will see you tomorrow night, then.'

'Yes, My Lord. Don't worry, I won't let you down!'

With these words, the ragged little man bowed and went away, leaving Llywelyn even more worried than before!

The second night's feast was as wonderful as the first. But Llywelyn did not eat much. He could not stop thinking about what would happen when people saw his ragged wizard.

Everyone in King John's court knew that the prince had agreed to arrange the entertainment, and they wanted to see if he could do as well as their king.

Llywelyn looked around. At the bottom of the hall, the little red-haired man was waiting. Llywelyn felt a bit sick, but he nodded to his new wizard, hoping that, somehow, it would be all right.

The ragged red-haired man stepped out into the space between the tables. He did not look like a wizard. As Llywelyn had expected, people began to laugh.

The little red-haired man bowed to his prince, and looked up at him to ask, 'Shall I begin, My Lord?'

Llywelyn nodded. The red-haired man lifted his arm and moved it slowly through the air.

Suddenly, they were sitting around a sea, with shoals of fish and a fleet of small ships, full of tiny sailors. Although the hall was full of water, no one had wet feet. They all clapped. It was the same magic that the Wizard of England had made.

The little red-haired man moved his arm, and ships, sails, fish and sea were all gone in the blink of an eye. Then he moved his arm again.

This time, a forest of tiny trees grew quickly in the space between the tables. Soon their branches hung down over cool glades. Wild pigs trotted in and began to snuffle around between the roots of the trees, searching for acorns. Then there was the sound of a horn, and hunters ran in with dogs and spears. They chased a pig, caught it and killed it. Then

They were sitting
around a sea.

they lit a fire in the glade, cut the meat into chunks and cooked it in an iron pot.

This all happened so quickly that the food was ready almost as soon as the hunt ended. The hunters carried the hot pot to each table and served everyone with stew. Even though they had only just finished a feast, the stew smelled so delicious that everyone tried it, and they all said it tasted wonderful.

When the pot was empty, the hunters bowed low to Prince Llywelyn, Princess Siwan and King John. Then they picked up their weapons, called their dogs and left the hall. The little red-haired man moved his arm, and the forest disappeared.

Everyone clapped and cheered as the little man bowed to his prince, looking up at him as if to ask, 'Are you pleased, My Lord?'

Llywelyn nodded and smiled. He was delighted.

King John turned to him and said, 'Your wizard has pleased everyone.'

But the king was wrong about that. One person was not pleased. The Wizard of

England stepped out in the space between the tables. His face was red with rage. How could this ragged fellow do such great magic – greater than his own?

In a temper, the wizard pointed at the ragged man, and started to spin a spell. But the red-haired man was quicker. He reached out his arm – and suddenly, the wizard was gone! Instead, a deer stood there, huge antlers on its head, looking around in fear.

Now the hunters ran in again, surrounded the deer and killed it. There was a gasp of horror from the people in the hall. But the hunters took no notice. They took out their knives and skinned the deer. They gave the deerskin to the ragged man. Then he moved his arm. The hunters and the body of the deer disappeared. But the red-haired man still held the deerskin. He lifted it high in the air. Then he dropped it.

Before it could touch the floor, it changed. The Wizard of England stood there, with a very puzzled look on his face. Everyone shouted with relief, and then began to clap and cheer for the red-haired man's magic.

A kind servant took the confused wizard by the arm and led him away. The ragged man bowed low, then walked quietly out of the hall.

King John turned to Llywelyn and Siwan and said, 'Your Welsh wizard has done well. I can see we will have good entertainment every night!'

'Your Majesty,' said Siwan, 'we will enjoy your English magic as much as you will enjoy our Welsh magic. Please ask your wizard to come back tomorrow. Tell him I am looking forward to seeing him again.'

So each night, the wizards took turns to show off their marvellous magic.

When he was not busy entertaining the English court, the ragged man made a magic palace for Llywelyn and Siwan, with fountains, pools and gardens, and forests full of singing birds. They stayed there happily all through the holiday, until the twelve days of Christmas were over, and it was time to come home to Wales.

Then King John asked, 'Will you give me your palace? After all, you can't take it back to Wales with you!'

But the red-haired man opened his hand and pulled the palace, the garden, the pools, the fountains and the forests into a little lump no bigger than a nut. Siwan smiled and put it in her pocket. And then they all came back to Wales.

At last they saw their dear Conwy valley, and knew they were nearly home. When they had crossed the river Conwy, the red-haired man came to Llywelyn and bowed low.

'I will say goodbye now, My Lord,' he said. 'You do not need me anymore.'

'Don't go!' said Llywelyn. 'Come to our palace. You will have a place of honour there.'

'Thank you, My Lord, but no. My home is in the forest. I came when you needed me, and now that you do not need me anymore, I am going home.'

And the little red-haired, bare-legged man turned and disappeared among the trees.

Llywelyn and Siwan never saw him again. But they never forgot him. Every Christmas they asked their storyteller to tell the story of the prince's wizard. It was Siwan's favourite story.

15

THE KING OF THE GIANTS

Once upon a time, when kings were kings and giants were really *big*, the King of the Giants had his court on the banks of the river Alyn, near where the town of Wrexham is now.

The giant's court was famous for feasts, entertainments and tournaments. Knights came from far and near to take part in jousting competitions and prove their strength. The prizes were fantastic, too: bags of gold for the winners, as well as a celebration feast and a special praise song about you, composed by the Giant Bard.

King Arthur's court at Camelot was not far from the giant's court, and one day Arthur called for five of his best knights.

'Boys,' said King Arthur, 'the King of the Giants is having a tournament to celebrate the birth of his giant baby daughter. Go to the competition and do your best, for the honour of the Knights of the Round Table.'

Sir Bedwyr, Sir Bors, Sir Cai, Sir Gawain and Sir Lancelot bowed to their king. Their hearts were full of excitement. They rushed away to pack what they needed – that didn't take long – and to polish their armour until it shone – that took quite a lot longer.

The next day they set out, and all the knights and ladies of King Arthur's court were there to cheer and wish them luck.

When they got near the Giant King's court, they saw flags waving in the wind and heard the excited chatter of hundreds of giants, queuing up for good seats to watch the jousts.

At last the competition began: knights in shining armour, war horses with long tails, trumpeters and judges and squires in the

Giant King's colourful livery, giant ladies and lords in their bright clothes watching from covered seats and ordinary giants in their best outfits cheering from the stands.

Arthur's knights were ready to do their best. And they did! Time after time, the herald announced, 'Victory to the knight of King Arthur!'

At the end of the day they were the champion team. That evening, they sat at the high table, beside the Giant King and Queen. They were served before everyone else, and the Giant Bard sang of their triumph. It was a wonderful night! And a long one …

They meant to get up early and set off home before the roads got too crowded. But they had stayed up very late. So they got up very late. By the time they had packed everything, saddled their horses, stuffed the prize bags of gold safely into their saddlebags and then said goodbye to all their new friends, it was nearly lunchtime.

Lancelot said, 'We might as well have lunch before we go. We don't want to get hungry on the way.'

They took off the horses' saddles and bridles and fed and watered them. They had a giant lunch and then a little rest.

By the time they saddled the horses again and set out at last, it was halfway through the afternoon. They enjoyed the ride along the bank of the river and across the valley, chatting and laughing as their horses ambled slowly along.

They made good time over the flat land of the Marches, the place where Wales meets England. But when evening came, they were still on the road. Now the path was not very clear, and because they were chatting, they were not careful about making sure they were going the right way.

Soon they were lost in the bog of Whixall Moss. It was getting dark, and the ground was soft and wet under the horses' hooves. They sank in with every step. The knights did not dare to stop to think about the way, in case they got completely stuck.

'We should dismount and lead our horses,' said Sir Lancelot. 'The gold in the saddlebags is heavy enough. We need to move as lightly as possible in this marsh, and find solid ground as soon as we can.'

The other knights did as Lancelot said, but they did not like the feeling of their feet sinking into the bog.

'Keep moving, friends,' said Lancelot. 'We don't want to be stuck here all night, do we?'

This only made everyone feel worse. If they were still there in the morning, would they be alive or dead?

They needed to keep going, but they didn't know which way to go. They were horribly lost, with mist all around them and the long night still ahead.

They stumbled on, cold, frightened and wet, leading their poor horses through the boggy ground.

Suddenly, an enormous red mouth opened in front of them! It was full of pointed teeth and from it came a terrible roar. The knights and their horses were terrified.

Then they saw more: it was not a mouth without a body, as it had first seemed to be.

It was a huge white lion.

It was a huge white lion. Its eyes were red and so were its ears.

Back then, everyone knew that a white animal with red eyes and red ears was a fairy creature. The knights thought that a magical beast was even more frightening than a wild animal.

But the lion did not attack them. Instead, it walked away for a few steps, then turned its shaggy head to look at them over its shoulder with its red eyes.

'It … it wants us to follow it,' said Sir Cai. 'Will it lead us to doom?'

'Or out of this terrible place?' said Lancelot.

The knights turned to look at him. 'Perhaps the Giant King has sent this lion to help us,' he said. 'Don't you remember that there is a white lion on his shield?'

This was true, and the knights looked again at the lion standing in the dark. It was swishing its tail from side to side, waiting for them to follow.

'Very well,' decided Lancelot, 'let us trust the lion. In truth, we have no choice. We are well and truly lost, and without help we will never find our way home. Here is help. Let's take it.'

He began to plod after the lion, which seemed to float easily over the bog.

The other knights followed nervously. But they did not need to worry. The white lion moved ahead, stopping now and again to look over its shoulder, to check that they were all still there. The wind of the marsh was cold behind them, but they only looked in front, at the shining lion.

At last they felt dry ground under their feet. They looked around. For the first time in a long time, they knew where they were. They recognised a familiar track, which led towards Camelot.

The lion took a few more steps, and then turned to look at them. Once more it opened its red mouth and roared. But now they were not afraid of it. They cheered in thanks, and the horses neighed gratefully too. In all that noise, the lion's voice was the loudest. Then suddenly, it was gone! The knights' voices died away too, in surprise: the lion had vanished. There were not even any paw prints in the mud to show that it had been there.

'A magical creature,' said Sir Cai, 'and now we have seen the full power of the King of the Giants.'

'Yes, he knew we needed help, even though he is far away,' agreed Lancelot. 'He really is a great king ...'

The others nodded thoughtfully.

'When we reach Camelot, the storytellers will tell everyone about our victory in the tournament,' said Lancelot. 'But we must make sure that the King of the Giants and his lion are remembered in the stories. Without them, we would never have come safely home.'

And they began to gallop towards Arthur's court.

16

KING MARCH

Once upon a time, there was a king called King March. His castle was at Castellmarch on the Llŷn.

King March made fair laws and he looked after his kingdom well. Everyone was happy. Everyone, except the king …

King March had a secret. It made him feel unhappy. It made him feel different. His ears were the secret.

They weren't like your ears, or mine. They were like horse's ears: long and straight and covered with short, smooth, brown hair. They were very nice ears, really, but they were in the wrong place. They belonged on a horse's head, not a man's. They made King March feel different.

Some people love to feel different. But some hate it. King March hated his ears. He didn't want anyone to know he had horse's ears. He bought a special crown to cover them, and grew his hair very long.

His hair got too long.

It got so long that he couldn't see where he was going.

It got so long that it went in his mouth when he had his dinner.

He knew he had to have a haircut.

King March told Tomos the barber to cut his hair. This was the first time Tomos had ever been asked to cut the king's hair, even though he had been the King's Barber for years.

But before Tomos could even pick up his scissors, King March said, 'Tomos, I have a secret. When you cut my hair you will know my secret too. No one else must know! You must promise never, ever to tell anyone. If you break your promise, you will be in terrible trouble. Do you understand?'

Tomos was scared. But he nodded. 'I promise, Your Majesty,' he said.

'Very good,' said King March, and he took off his special crown.

Tomos began to cut the king's hair, and soon he saw his ears. But he didn't say a word, and just carried on cutting.

When Tomos finished, King March put back his special crown and looked in the mirror. He smiled and said, 'Well done, Tomos. Thank you. Now, don't forget your promise. You must never, ever tell anyone my secret.'

'I won't, Your Majesty,' said Tomos. He packed his things and went home.

But sometimes it is hard to keep a secret. Tomos couldn't stop thinking about King March's ears. He really wanted to tell someone about them. But he didn't dare. The secret began to make him feel ill. He couldn't eat. He couldn't sleep. His friends got worried about him.

'What's wrong, Tomos?' they asked.

'Nothing,' said Tomos.

But it wasn't true.

King March has horse's ears!

'Can't you tell me what's wrong?' asked his friend Bronwen one day.

'No,' said Tomos miserably. 'It's a secret. I promised I wouldn't tell.'

'Well, you mustn't break your promise,' said Bronwen.

'I know,' said Tomos, 'but I think I will burst if I don't tell someone. What can I do?'

Bronwen thought for a bit, and then she said, 'Why don't you go down to the river and whisper the secret to the reeds that grow there? Then you can say the secret out loud without breaking your promise. It might help.'

It sounded like a good idea, so Tomos went down to the river and knelt in the long reeds.

He whispered, 'King March has horse's ears! King March has horse's ears!'

He felt so much better that he said it again.

'King March has horse's ears!'

He jumped up. He felt great! That night he slept well for the first time in ages.

Then King March decided to have a big feast to celebrate his birthday. Everyone was invited: there would be good food and music for dancing.

On the day of the feast, musicians from all over Llŷn set out for Castellmarch. The flute player was called Beth. She was the best flute player of them all.

On her way she walked along the river-bank. When she saw the reeds, she thought, 'Those reeds would make lovely flutes. Maybe I should make a new flute to play for the king.'

So she chose a long strong reed and cut it to be her new flute. She was very pleased with it.

At King March's palace, the party began.

'Let's have some music,' said King March. 'Please give us a tune, Beth.'

Beth put her new flute to her lips and blew.

But the flute didn't play a tune. Instead, it whispered, 'King March has horse's ears! King March has horse's ears!'

Everyone looked at King March. King March looked at Beth.

'What's that?' he asked in an angry voice.

Beth's hands trembled as she lifted her flute and tried again.

'King March has horse's ears!' sang the flute. 'King March has horse's ears!'

King March's face was red. But before he could say any more, Tomos came to stand by Beth.

'Your Majesty,' he said. 'I couldn't keep your secret, so I told the reeds. It isn't Beth's fault. It's mine.'

'No it isn't,' said Bronwen, coming to stand next to him. 'Your Majesty, keeping your secret was making Tomos ill. I told him to whisper it to the reeds. It isn't his fault. It's mine.'

King March looked at Beth, Tomos and Bronwen. Then he sighed.

'It's true,' he said. 'I have got horse's ears. I've kept them a secret for too long. Look!'

He took off his special crown and pushed back his hair.

Everyone shouted: 'Our king has horse's ears! King March has horse's ears! He is special!'

'Special?' asked King March. 'Not different? Not strange?'

'No!' they shouted. 'You're special.'

And they all cheered.

'Oh,' said King March, looking pleased. 'Well, yes, I suppose I am. Hurray! Let's have some music!'

So Beth and the other musicians played, while Tomos and Bronwen and everyone else danced.

And from that day on, King March decided not to be ashamed of being different, but to be proud of being special.

17

THE CLOAK OF KINGS' BEARDS

Once upon a time, this land wasn't the way it is today: one united kingdom with one queen. Instead, there were lots of small kingdoms, and each small kingdom had a small king.

But there was one king who wasn't small at all … because he was a *giant*! His name was Rhita Fawr, which means Rhita the Big. It was a good name for a giant.

He was a greedy giant. He wanted lots of money, lots of power … and, especially, lots of land. So, every time he met one of the little kings, he would say, 'Look at my field. What a huge field it is!'

Well, the little king looked one way, he looked the other way … there are a lot of fields in Wales, as you know if you live here.

'Which one?' asked the little king. 'Which one is your huge field?'

'It's up there!' shouted the giant. 'The sky is my huge field!'

'Oh, that's nice,' said the little king politely, because it is never a good idea to argue with a giant.

'And look at your sheep,' yelled the giant, 'eating the grass in my field. And look at my shepherd, taking care of them for you!'

'Where are my sheep?' asked the puzzled little king.

Because there aren't any sheep in the sky, are there?

But there is something in the sky that looks a bit like sheep: the same colour, the same texture.

Can you guess what it is?

'The clouds are your sheep,' roared the giant, 'eating the grass in my field. And the sun is my shepherd, taking care of them for you.'

'Oh. Right,' said the little king.

'And you've got to pay me,' said the giant. 'You've got to pay the rent for the field, and you've got to pay the shepherd's wages.'

'Oh dear,' said the little king. 'How much is it?'

'Hmmm,' said the giant. 'Your kingdom will just about pay for using the field. And for the shepherd's wages … I'll take your beard!'

And he grabbed hold of the little king's beard and sliced it right off with his big sharp sword.

'The clouds are your sheep!'

You see, the giant had a cloak. It was a giant cloak, of course, because he was a giant, but it was very plain. It didn't have any buttons or bows, any ribbons or roses, any stripes or spots. So the giant had decided to decorate his cloak with a lovely beardy fringe. And because he was a king, and the cloak was a king's cloak, he only wanted kings' beards to decorate it.

It wasn't long before the whole land was full of small kings with no beards and no kingdoms. It wasn't long before the giant's kingdom was *enormous*! And it wasn't long before the giant's cloak had a lovely beardy fringe all around the edge.

There was just one little gap down at the bottom.

'Hmmm,' said the giant to himself one day, 'where can I find a king with a small beard to fit that gap?' He knew he needed a young king, with a beard that hadn't grown very big.

And then he heard about a new king in the land. A new king who was a young king – so a king with a small beard. A young king who had become king, by pulling a sword out of a stone.

Do you know that young king's name?

King Arthur. They call him The Once and Future King.

As soon as the giant had thought of King Arthur, he knew that Arthur's beard would be the perfect one to finish his cloak.

He wrote a note to King Arthur, 'Bring me your beard straight away!' He didn't even say please! He gave the note to his messenger and sent him to find King Arthur.

The giant's messenger arrived at King Arthur's court and gave him the message. Arthur read it and thought it was very rude. But he didn't blame the messenger. He knew the messenger had only carried the message. He hadn't written it.

Arthur replied politely, the way a king should, 'Please, go back to King Rhita, up there in North Wales, and tell him I will bring my beard to him, to save him the trouble of travelling.'

As soon as the messenger had left the court, Arthur spoke to his knights. They were, of course, all sitting at the Round Table.

'Get your swords,' he said quietly. 'Get your shields. Get your spears. Mount your horses. We are riding to the kingdom of that rude giant!'

While Arthur and the Knights of the Round Table were riding to North Wales, the giant was relaxing in his castle garden. The sun was shining, the air was warm, the birds were singing, the bees were buzzing. It was so peaceful that the giant was falling asleep.

Suddenly there was a flash of lightning. Next came a roll of thunder. And then, the giant smelled a sweet smell. A sweet, sweet smell carried on the wind.

He was puzzled. He called to his lookout to come down from the top of the tallest tower.

'What's going on?' asked the giant. 'Lightning on a sunny day? Thunder from a clear sky? A sweet, sweet smell carried on the wind? What's going on?'

'Your Majesty,' said the lookout. 'That flash you saw wasn't lightning. It was the sun shining on the swords of the knights of King Arthur, coming here to attack you!'

'Oh dear,' said the giant.

'And the sound you heard wasn't thunder,' said the lookout. 'That sound was the war cry of the knights of King Arthur, coming here to attack you!'

'Oh dear, oh dear,' said the giant.

'And the sweet smell is the smell of the magic potion that the knights of King Arthur drink before they fight. The magic potion that means they can never be beaten in battle.'

'Oh dear, oh dear, oh dear,' said the giant.

When King Arthur and his knights arrived, the cowardly giant gave up without a fight.

King Arthur looked at the giant. 'King Rhita,' he said, 'I can see just the beard you need to finish your cloak.'

King Arthur called for his barber, and the barber came running in with a razor, a shaving brush, a bowl of warm soapy water ... and a little ladder under his arm.

The barber set up his ladder in front of the giant and climbed to the top. This made him high enough to put plenty of bubbles on the giant's chin with his brush, and then to slice off the giant's own beard with his razor.

That made the giant mad! There was a bitter battle. At the end, it was the giant who lay dead on the ground.

'We must bury the giant,' said Arthur to his knights. 'It would be too hard to dig a big enough hole, so I want each one of you to bring a great grey stone to pile up over the body.'

The highest mountain in the land.

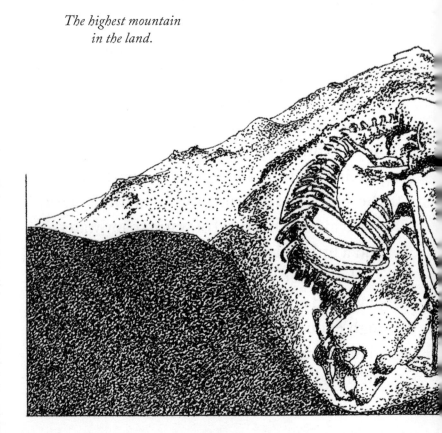

The knights brought great stones and piled them up until the giant was covered, and there was a mountain of stones.

A new mountain in the land. A high mountain. The highest mountain in the land.

That mountain is still there. In English the mountain is called Mount Snowdon. In Welsh it is called Yr Wyddfa, which in English means 'the burial place'.

Hundreds of people go there every year. They walk on that mountain. They climb on it. They ride up to the top on the little train and have a cup of tea in the cafe.

But how many of them know what you know, and I know?

Under the grass …

and the earth …

and the rocks …

and the stones …

lie the long white bones of the giant.

18

KING ARTHUR'S HORSE

Once upon a time, King Arthur had a castle at the top of one of Flintshire's round-topped hills. The hill is still called Moel Arthur, which means Arthur's round-topped hill, of course.

From the top of his hill, King Arthur could see far across the land, and keep his people safe.

In those days there was a lot of trouble from invaders, and Arthur had to be ready at any time to defend the land, with the help of his knights, the Knights of the Round Table.

One day, a messenger brought bad news to Arthur: an enemy army was on its way to attack the kingdom.

'Off we go, boys!' said Arthur to the knights. 'We must defend the land!'

The two armies met on the Clwydian Hills. From sunrise to sunset there was nothing to hear except the clash of iron weapons.

Suddenly, Arthur found himself in terrible trouble. His enemies were surrounding him and he could not see his own people anywhere. He was all alone in the middle of his enemies – all alone except for his wonderful horse, of course.

'Llamrei,' he said to his horse, 'save us both!'

Off went Llamrei like lightning, with enemies following close behind. Arthur could see death all around him, and most especially right in front of him, because Llamrei was galloping straight towards the edge of a high cliff.

But Arthur trusted his marvellous horse, and he was right to trust him.

Llamrei raced straight at the cliff and jumped off, into the wild white air, and then he and Arthur began to fall down … and down … and down …

Llamrei jumped off the cliff.

The enemies all screeched to a halt, just before they fell over the edge themselves. They looked down, expecting to see the dead bodies of the king and his horse. But instead they saw Arthur galloping away, waving goodbye to them with a big grin on his face! He was quite safe, and all ready for the next battle, wherever it might be.

Llamrei had saved his royal rider, landing from that great height with such force that his two front hooves sank deep into a rock at the bottom of the cliff. That rock is still there, and it is now the marker stone showing where Flintshire begins.

It is called Carreg Carn March Arthur, which means the Stone with the Footprint of Arthur's Horse, because you can still see the marks that Llamrei made when he landed. People who live in Flintshire say that this is proof that Arthur lived there once, long ago.

19

BRANWEN'S BIRD

Branwen had four brothers. One of them was a giant. His name was Bran. Bran was the king of the Island of the Mighty, and Branwen was the most beautiful maiden in the kingdom. Her name means 'White Raven', and she loved birds of all kinds.

One day she was watching the seagulls gliding over the sea, sitting on the cliff at Harlech with her four brothers. Beside Branwen was her brother Bran, the king. Next to him was Manawydan, their thoughtful brother. And next to him were Nisien and Efnisien, who were like day and night … or black and white … or wrong and right. Nisien was a peacemaker. He was easy to live with. Efnisien was a troublemaker. He was *not* easy to live with!

'Look at the ships!' said Branwen suddenly, pointing out to sea.

They watched thirteen ships come to shore. The king of Ireland jumped out of the first one. He looked up at Branwen sitting on the cliffs, and called out, 'Branwen, I have come to ask you to marry me! If you do, there will always be peace between Wales and Ireland. What do you say?'

Branwen looked at her brothers. 'I don't even know him,' she said, 'but peace is a good thing. I'll think about this.'

Three of them looked pleased. They wanted peace. Only Efnisien was not pleased. He liked trouble best!

Well, they had a wedding. And after the wedding, they had a feast.

Everyone was happy. Everyone except for Efnisien. He only wanted trouble, so he made trouble. Big trouble. He went to the stables where the Irish king's horses were kept, and he cut them with a sharp, cruel knife. He cut every single one of them.

The king of Ireland was really upset. And angry. He was ready to go home to Ireland and leave Branwen behind, because of her troublesome brother. But Bran made peace. He gave the king of Ireland fine new horses, and gold and silver. And then he gave him something even more precious: he gave him the Cauldron of Rebirth.

'It was brought to Wales from Ireland by two giants,' Bran told the king. 'Now I'll give it back to you. If you put dead warriors into it, they will come back to life. You will never be beaten in battle now.'

The king of Ireland was pleased by Bran's generous gifts. So peace was made, and Branwen sailed to Ireland with her new husband.

When she arrived, Branwen gave everyone presents and they all welcomed her as their new queen.

For a year, she was happy.

The next year, she was even happier. She had a baby boy. She named him Gwern.

But after three years, things began to go wrong. It was as if Efnisien could make trouble even when he was far away. No-one could forget the trouble he had made at Branwen's wedding. They couldn't forgive him, and they put the blame on Branwen.

'That troublemaker is far away,' people said to the king, 'but his sister is right here. You should not have married her. We don't want her as our queen.'

The king listened to them. He let them persuade him that what Efnisien had done was somehow Branwen's fault.

He gave his orders, 'Take away her crown. Take away her throne. Take away her fine clothes. Take away our baby, Gwern. She will not be his mother anymore. She will not be the queen anymore.

'Give her rags to wear. Give her scraps to eat. Send her to work in the kitchen. And tell the butcher to slap her face every night, on his way home from work. We will punish Branwen for the trouble her brother made.'

So a bad time began for Branwen. The food was horrible. The work was hard. The butcher was cruel. She missed her baby very much.

She was lonely: far from home, far from her brothers. She had nobody to be her friend.

Until, one day, a little bird landed on the window sill of the kitchen, next to where she was making bread. It was a starling. It chirped as if it wanted to talk to her. She couldn't understand what it was trying to say, but its song made her smile. She talked to it, and put crumbs on the window sill for it to eat.

The next day it came back. And the next day. And the day after that. Every day Branwen saved food for the starling. Every day she talked to it and it talked to her. Little by little, they began to understand each other.

Branwen thought, 'I have a friend. She is only a little bird, but she is my friend.'

And then she thought, 'Maybe the bird can help me!'

Branwen could not leave the castle. She could not go to Wales and ask her giant brother Bran for help. 'But the bird could go for me!' she thought. 'The bird could fly over the sea to Wales, and find Bran, and give him a letter from me!'

It was hard to explain all this to the bird. But the bird chirped happily. She was ready to help.

Branwen found a little scrap of paper. She wrote, 'Bran, I need help. Come and rescue me. Your sister, Branwen.'

There wasn't room to write more. The paper had to be very small, because the bird couldn't carry much. Branwen folded the scrap of paper. She tied it under the bird's wing with one of her long red-gold hairs. She stood by the open window with the bird in her hands.

'Go safely, little friend,' she whispered. 'Cross the sea and find my brother. Thank you for helping me.'

She lifted her hands and launched the bird into the sky.

The little bird chirped and flew away towards the seashore. She was not a sea bird. She had never flown over the waves. But now she did. She did it for Branwen.

It was a hard journey. The wind was strong. The air was cold. The sea raged below her, rain and hail beat down on her and fish leapt up towards her into the air. But she kept going.

She launched the bird into the sky.

At last she saw misty mountains and heard the sound of waves breaking on the shore.

She flew over the waves, over the beach. She landed on the first tree she found, and she rested. But not for long.

Soon she was flying again, searching for the giant king. She found him on the island of Anglesey. He was there with his court, but he was not in a castle. There was no castle in Wales big enough for Branwen's giant brother, so he was sitting on a small hill in the open air, with people all around him.

The bird flew down and fluttered round his huge head. She perched on his massive shoulder. She pecked at his enormous ear.

She was so small and he was so big that the giant didn't notice her at first. He didn't notice her until she landed on his hand and jumped up and down, squawking and chirping and making as much noise as she could.

Bran lifted his hand to his face and peered at the little dot. She flapped her wings hard, to show him the letter that Branwen had tied under one of them.

Someone with smaller hands had to untie the letter and unfold it. Someone with smaller eyes had to read it out to Bran. 'Bran, I need help. Come and rescue me. Your sister, Branwen.'

When he heard that, Bran shouted, 'Get ships ready! Get soldiers ready! We have to rescue my sister!'

The little bird knew she could rest now. She had done what Branwen had asked her to do.

The ships were ready. Soldiers went on board. Sailors pulled up the anchors.

The bird watched. She was too tired to fly across the sea again, but she wished she could see Branwen.

She saw that Bran was still on land. He was too big to travel in a ship. He waded into the sea. He shouted, 'We won't wait for the wind. Throw me the ropes!'

From each ship a long rope was thrown to Bran. He began to walk towards Ireland, pulling the ships behind him.

Suddenly, the little bird took off. She flew to Bran and perched on his shoulder. 'Are you coming too, little bird?' asked Bran. 'Well, I can easily carry you. Let's go to Ireland!'

Bran walked across the sea to Ireland, pulling his ships.

The king of Ireland heard people shouting. He asked, 'What's the matter?'

A man said, 'Your Majesty, something very strange is happening. A mountain is coming across the sea. It has a long ridge with two big lakes, one on each side of the ridge. There is a forest all around it.'

'A mountain? A forest? Coming over the sea? That doesn't make sense,' said the king.

'If you knew my brother, it would make sense,' shouted Branwen from the kitchen. 'That forest is the masts of his ships. The mountain is my brother Bran. The long ridge is his nose and the two big lakes are his eyes. He is coming to set me free, and when he gets here you will be sorry!'

The king of Ireland knew he had been wrong to treat Branwen so badly, and he was afraid. 'We don't want to fight,' he said. 'We'll leave the castle and cross the river. Break down all the bridges after we cross, so that Bran and his army cannot follow us.'

When Bran reached the castle, there was no-one there. The little bird chirped, and flew away to find Branwen. Bran and his army followed her. When they reached the river, the bird flew over, but the soldiers could not cross.

So Bran said, 'The one who is a leader should be a bridge.'

He lay down across the river, and all the warriors with all the weapons marched across his back.

When the king of Ireland heard this, he said, 'We can't fight them. We must make peace. Peace is better than trouble.'

He sent a messenger to Bran to ask for peace.

As Bran listened to the messenger, the little bird flew from his shoulder. Branwen reached out her hands, and the bird landed.

'Welcome back, little friend,' said Branwen. 'Thank you. Thank you for bringing my brother. Thank you for helping me. Now we can all be together again.'

And the two kings made peace.

THE TALE OF TALIESIN

Once upon a time a man called Tegid lived by a lake with his wife and their two children. In English, the lake is called Bala Lake, and it has the same name as the little town beside it. In Welsh, it is called Llyn Tegid, named for the Tegid in this story.

Tegid's wife's name was Ceridwen, and she was a Woman of Power.

Their daughter was beautiful, very beautiful. In fact, she was so beautiful that she falls right out of the story, and I can't tell you anything else about her at all. Sorry.

But their son was so mean and moany, so grumpy and groany, that even his mother could see that life was going to be hard for him. Because Ceridwen was a Woman of Power, she decided to use her magic to do something about this.

She looked in all her books of magic until she found the spell she wanted. It was a spell to make her son wise and inspiring.

'If he is wise,' she thought, 'who will mind if he is moany? If he is inspiring, who will care if he is groany?'

The spell was to make a magic potion. It needed to cook for a year and a day. At the end of that time, there would be three magic drops in the potion. Whoever drank the three drops would know everything!

Ceridwen started to make the spell.

She took her iron cauldron down to the lake and filled it with water. She made a fire and put the cauldron on the fire to boil and bubble, for a year and a day. She found an old man to put wood on the fire, to keep it burning for a year and a day. And she found a little boy to stir the pot and keep it from sticking and burning, for a year and a day.

The boy's name was Gwion. Gwion's work was hard, hot and boring. His job was to stir the pot, while Ceridwen collected the ingredients for the spell: roots and shoots, berries and fruits … each one picked at the right time of year, the right time of day …

The more she put in the pot, the thicker the mixture got. It was hard for Gwion to turn the spoon and stir the pot. But he knew he must not let it stick and burn. Ceridwen would be angry with him. It was not a good idea to make her angry!

Spring turned to summer while Gwion stirred the pot.

Summer turned to autumn while Gwion stirred the pot.

Autumn turned to winter while Gwion stirred the pot.

Finally, winter turned to spring again. Gwion was still stirring the pot.

A whole year had passed, and only one day was needed for the three magic drops to be ready.

That day was the day when the trouble started. I don't know why Ceridwen wasn't there when it happened.

This is what happened: a giant bubble floated up to the top of the pot. It burst with a loud 'pop!' on the top of the mixture. Big hot drops splashed everywhere. Three drops splashed on Gwion's hand, where he held the spoon and stirred the pot. Those three drops were hot! Hot with the boiling of a year and a day.

Gwion yelped, and jumped back. He put his cool tongue on his poor burnt hand. When he did that, he licked up the three magic drops that Ceridwen had been cooking all year for her son.

Suddenly, Gwion knew everything. He knew that Ceridwen would be angry with him, and that she would come after him. He dropped the spoon that he had held for a whole year, and he ran away as fast as he could.

Wherever she was, Ceridwen did know. She knew that Gwion had the magic she had been making for her son. She was angry. Very angry. She came after him at full speed.

He ran and she ran.

She ran and he ran.

Soon he could hear her getting closer.

He could see her running, when he looked over his shoulder: getting closer.

He could hear her feet slapping against the ground: getting closer.

He knew he couldn't outrun her. But he could use his new magic power … he changed his shape, and became the fastest animal he could think of.

He became a hare, with long ears and strong legs, racing away over the hill.

But Ceridwen had magic power too. She

He became a hare and she became a hound.

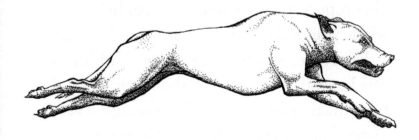

changed her shape too. She became a grey-hound, a racing dog, just as long and strong as the hare: running after him, getting closer.

The hare that was Gwion looked back along his grey, furry side. He knew that, even as a hare, he could not escape from her.

So he changed again. The hare jumped up, and splashed down in the water of Bala Lake. As he went in, he became a fish, with silver scales and a strong tail, flashing through the water.

The greyhound never missed a step. It leapt into the water after him.

As she entered the water, Ceridwen changed too. She became an otter, a fast-swimming animal that swims as swiftly as a fish – and eats fish too, tearing them to pieces with its needle-sharp teeth.

The fish that was Gwion looked back along his silver-scaled side. He knew that, even as a fish, he could not escape from her.

So he changed again. The fish gave a leap, and as it left the water it became a bird, its little wings beating fast, its little heart beating fast too.

But the otter changed again too. She jumped out of the water and became an eagle, with strong claws and cruel beak, and flew after him.

They changed and changed again.

The little bird that was Gwion looked back over his desperate flapping wings. He knew that, even as a bird, he could not escape from her. He looked around for somewhere to hide.

He saw a farm, near the shore of the lake. The farmer had cut his corn and the good golden grains were heaped up in the farmyard. The little bird dropped from the air like a stone.

When he landed in the farmyard he changed again.

Gwion became a golden grain of corn in a heap of thousands of grains of corn, all exactly the same.

But the eagle flew down too, and landed in the farmyard. As she reached the ground, Ceridwen changed her shape. She became a big black hen, with a yellow beak and yellow claws. She scratched and scritched, and pecked and picked, until she found the grain of corn that was Gwion.

She pecked him up and swallowed him down, into her crop.

He stayed there.

But he didn't die.

When Ceridwen changed back into her own true shape, Gwion was still there, in her belly.

As the days passed and turned to weeks, and the weeks passed and turned to months, Ceridwen's belly began to swell. Soon everyone could see that she was going to have a baby.

But when the baby was born, Ceridwen didn't want to keep him, because she knew he would always remind her of what her other son had lost.

So she put the new baby into a bag made of the skins of birds, and took him down to the seashore at Aberdyfi, where the river Dyfi flows into the sea. She bent down and put the baby in the bag into the water. The tide carried him out to sea.

The wind and the waves rocked the baby in the bag in just the same way that mothers and fathers rock babies in their arms. The baby was rocked by the wind and the waves for years and years. The tides carried him here and there. But all the time the baby was in the bag he was never hungry, never thirsty, he never cried and he never got even one day older.

At last, after a long, long time, the wind and the waves brought the baby in the bag back to the place where the river Dyfi flows into the sea. The waves carried the baby up the river to a pool where the sweet water of the river mixed with the salt water of the sea. When the waves rolled out again, the baby in the bag was left in the pool, caught in the roots of a tree. For the first time in a long, long time, the baby in the bag was still.

That pool was the best place in Wales for catching fish. It belonged to the king. The king had given it to his son. The prince went there to fish. He threw his net into the water, but when he pulled it out it was empty, except for a bag tangled up in the net.

The prince took out the bag and looked at it.

'I wonder what's inside,' he said to himself. 'Perhaps there is gold or treasure.'

He opened the bag, trying to guess what he would see. He did not expect to see a baby inside it. But there was a baby! The baby's face was shining with wisdom and inspiration from the three drops of magic potion.

'Oh,' said the prince. 'What a shining face!'

But of course, he said this in Welsh, and the old Welsh words that mean 'shining face' are 'tal iesin'.

So the new baby got a new name. He wasn't Gwion any more. He was Taliesin, and that has been his name ever since.

Taliesin had all the wisdom and inspiration that the three magic drops had given to Gwion. Even though he was only a baby, he could tell stories and make up poems. He told stories and made up poems for the prince all the way back from the river Dyfi to the king's court. He told stories and made up poems for the king when they reached the court. Everyone was amazed by his words.

The king said, 'I will make Taliesin the Chief Poet of my court.'

Even today, people still remember Taliesin's poems, and they tell this story about him.

Bee bo bendit,
This story has ended.
If you don't like it,
Come to Wales,
Get copper nails
And mend it!

Snip, snap, snout,
All my stories are out.

THANKS

With thanks to William, Alex and Leo Raichura; to their mum, storyteller Katy Cawkwell; to storyteller June Peters; and to everyone in Mrs Mollison-White's class at Ysgol Carrog in July 2015, for advice and help with this book.

Thanks also to my editor at The History Press, Nicola Guy. And a big Diolch yn fawr iawn to Ed for the pictures.

The stories in this book are all part of the oral tradition, which means many different people have been telling them, for a long time. They don't 'belong' to one person in the way that an authored story does, and can be heard from many storytellers, as well as found in many books. But I would like to express my special thanks for four stories to the people who told them to me. Without their help I would not know these stories.

So, thank you to:

Teleri Jarman, for permission to translate her mother Eldra's story, 'Three Wishes', into English from Welsh;

Esyllt Harker, for 'Hen Wen the Pig' and 'The Prince's Wizard', both of which she found in old books and told to me;

Dez and Ali Quarréll for telling me about 'The King of the Giants'.

Society *for*
Storytelling

Since 1993, The Society for Storytelling has championed the ancient art of oral storytelling and its long and honourable history – not just as entertainment, but also in education, health, and inspiring and changing lives. Storytellers, enthusiasts and academics support and are supported by this registered charity to ensure the art is nurtured and developed throughout the UK.

Many activities of the Society are available to all, such as locating storytellers on the Society website, taking part in our annual National Storytelling Week at the start of every February, purchasing our quarterly magazine Storylines, or attending our Annual Gathering – a chance to revel in engaging performances, inspiring workshops, and the company of like-minded people.

You can also become a member of the Society to support the work we do. In return, you receive free access to Storylines, discounted tickets to the Annual Gathering and other storytelling events, the opportunity to join our mentorship scheme for new storytellers, and more. Among our great deals for members is a 30% discount off titles from The History Press.

For more information, including how to join, please visit

www.sfs.org.uk